BY THE SAME AUTHOR

Novels
Mrs. Martin's Man
Alice and a Family
Changing Winds
The Foolish Lovers

Plays
The Magnanimous Lover
Mixed Marriage
Jane Clegg
John Ferguson
The Ship
Mary, Mary, Quite Contrary
The Lady of Belmont
Anthony and Anna
Sauce for the Goose

Short Stories
Eight O'Clock and Other Studies

Political Studies
Sir Edward Carson and the Ulster
    Movement
Parnell

Personal Essays
Some Impressions of My Elders

Theatre Craft
The Organised Theatre

THE WAYWARD MAN

The WAYWARD MAN

By
ST. JOHN G ERVINE

NEW YORK
THE MACMILLAN COMPANY
1927

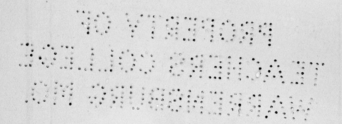

TO

LEONORA

THE FIRST PART

OF

THE WAYWARD MAN

News from a foreign country came
  As if my treasure and my wealth lay there;
So much it did my heart inflame,
    'Twas wont to call my Soul into mine ear;
      Which thither went to meet
      The approaching sweet,
      And on the threshold stood
      To entertain the unknown Good.
        It hover'd there
      As if 'twould leave mine ear,
      And was so eager to embrace
      The joyful tidings as they came,
    'Twould almost leave its dwelling-place
      To entertain the same.
                    THOMAS TRAHERNE.

THE WAYWARD MAN

THE FIRST CHAPTER

I

THE Terrace, which stood a short distance down
Pottinger's Road from the new bridge over the Lagan,
contained three shops, four parlour-houses, and a house
which was neither one thing nor the other. In this
last lived Mr. Lynas, the tailor. The front of his house
looked like that of any other parlour-house, but if a
passer-by had peeped through the window he would
have seen, not, as he might have expected, a small
d'oyley-covered table, bearing a pot of geraniums or
perhaps a brass-bound Bible or a full-rigged ship inside
a narrow bottle, but a counter bearing bales of cloth
and possibly Mr. Lynas, who used to say to his neighbours that one of these days he really would have to
ask Mr. Peden, the landlord, to give him a shop-front.
But despite the promptings of his wife, an ambitious
woman who resented the half-and-half appearance of
her husband's business, Mr. Lynas never made the
request, and when at last Mr. Peden, thinking of higher
rents, resolved to convert all the parlour-houses into
shops, Mr. Lynas was so angry that he abruptly
departed from the Terrace to another part of the town
and passed out of the knowledge of his neighbours.

1

The Terrace lay between Portugal Street and Modesty Row, and the order of its shops and houses was this. First, at the corner of Pottinger's Road and Portugal Street came Mr. Peden's Italian warehouse which was celebrated for two things: that it was the largest shop in the Terrace and that it was the business place of the man who owned the Terrace. Next to Mr. Peden's shop came Mrs. Dunwoody's, a dull and tiresome shop, her son Robert thought, with hardly a glimmer of glory in it. She dealt in hardware and delf and lamp-oil and brushes and a variety of things which were undoubtedly useful and necessary but could not be called either edible or enthralling. The Mineelys, now, on the other side of the street—people who did not live in the Terrace at all!—sold newspapers and sweets. There was a trade to engage the mind and the appetite! Robert many times flattened his nose until it was white against the Mineelys' window, and filled his thoughts with the wonders of a life spent in such surroundings. He could eat and read, read and eat! "And where would the profit be on that?" his elder brother Alec once wisely demanded. "Och, profit!" Robert roared with such scorn that Alec shrivelled away, murmuring, "Well, somebody has to think of them things sometimes!" There was always a large tray in the centre of the Mineelys' window, on which red and white cokernut chips were piled in a high heap, and Robert, who liked cokernut chips next to preserved ginger, would feel a sick envy of Jamesey Mineely who had had the good luck to be born of parents possessing so delectable a business. His faith in God had been badly shaken when a long and earnest prayer that his mother might be persuaded to give up

the sale of hardware and take to the sale of confec-
tionery and papers remained unanswered. . . .

Following Mrs. Dunwoody's shop came the four
parlour-houses, all of which were dull to look at, and,
except the third, dully occupied. The exceptional
parlour-house was inhabited by the Cairnduffs. Mrs.
Cairnduff's father had been a Presbyterian minister in
Derry, and she was considered to have married beneath
her when she espoused the master of a small sailing-
ship which tramped about the oceans of the world;
but Mrs. Cairnduff did not share this opinion, nor
could any one make her realise how she had fallen in
society, so, after a while, no one tried. "Anyway, the
woman's happy," was the conclusion to which people
came when they talked about her marriage. She had
one daughter, Brenda, who frequently wore a white
dress on Sundays and was the first girl in the Terrace
to be seen wearing brown stockings. She was strictly
forbidden to play with the rough children in Modesty
Row. Her playmates, among whom Alec and Robert
Dunwoody were included, were carefully chosen by her
mother so that there might be no chance of roughness
coming into her conduct or her conversation. She
always said, "I did so," when commoner children
would have said, "I did." This was considered to be
a great piece of refinement. She never said "Aye"; she
always said "Yes." She called her mother "mamma"
and her father "papa." She wore a white petticoat
every day.

Alec was very fond of Brenda, but Robert liked to
play with her only when her father was home from one
of his long voyages.

"Do you think your da would tell us about his

trips?" he would say to Brenda, who would reply first, "I wish you wouldn't say 'Da,' Darkie!" and then, "I dare say!" Everybody called Robert "Darkie Dunwoody" because he was the only member of his family who had not got very fair hair.

"Och, sure, what's wrong with 'da'?" Darkie once demanded.

"It's common," said Brenda.

"You're always talkin' about common things," he complained.

"Well, I don't like common things or common people," she retorted.

Robert did not care much about Brenda—"She's a weeshy-weeshy sort of a girl," he told himself; but she liked him better than any other boy, and she begged her father to tell them a story of his trips abroad because she knew that then Robert would contentedly sit beside her, without wanting, at the end of a few minutes, to run away.

"It's funny you can't content yourself like Alec," she said to him once when he was restless. "Alec'll sit beside me as long as I'll let him."

"Och, Alec!" Robert replied, laughing at his brother. "Sure, he's an oul' Jenny-jo."

"You shouldn't talk that way about your brother!"

"An', forby, he's coortin' you," continued Robert, ignoring her interruption.

Brenda flushed and looked away. "You're awfully common sometimes," she said.

II

Mr. Lynas's half-and-half shop-and-house succeeded to the four parlour-houses, and was succeeded, last in the Terrace, by Mr. Scarlett's shop. Mr. Peden's shop began the Terrace; Mr. Scarlett's shop ended it; and these were the two that interested Robert. The fact that they were described as the first and last was in itself sufficiently interesting. He remembered a cryptic reference to the first and the last in the Bible which had mystified him until he began to imagine that it might be explained in terms of Mr. Peden and Mr. Scarlett. It had mystified him because public-houses, notoriously kept by Roman Catholics, were sometimes called "The First and the Last," and he knew, for his mother had been careful to impress the fact on his mind, that public-houses were not reconcilable with the Word of God even when they were kept by Protestants. It was conceivable, as she suggested, that the reason why so many publicans were Catholics was because persons of that faith were forbidden by the priests to read the Bible for themselves, but she did not profess to understand these things. It was enough for her that there was a hint of hell in "The First and the Last," and everybody knew that the shortest way to damnation was through a public-house. It was also enough for her that Protestants believed in the Open Bible—a model of which was generally to be found dangling from Orange arches on the Twelfth of July—though, indeed, when she thought about it she realised that there were things in the Good Book which were better not talked about too loudly or too often. She *had* heard that a public-house was sometimes called "The First and the Last" for a reason unconnected with the Scripture, because it was the first to be encountered by countrymen coming into the town and the last to be passed on the way out again—thus giving them timely opportunity to get drunk both ways! . . .

But there were other and profounder reasons than these for Robert's delight in the first and the last shops in the Terrace. They had an air of romance which was missing from his mother's shop. Mr. Peden's was romantically named and it was bigger than Mrs. Dunwoody's. Robert could not understand why it was called an Italian warehouse, for there seemed to be no difference between it and any other grocery, but he did not greatly trouble himself with explanations. That it was called Italian was sufficient for him, and he would open his atlas and gaze at the boot-shaped map of Italy, with its heel in the Adriatic and its toe almost touching the rump of Sicily, and tell himself that it was next door. There was a volcano in Italy, and Robert would not in the least have been astonished if it had suddenly erupted in the middle of Mr. Peden's shop. The main entrance to the Italian warehouse was neatly placed on the corner, so that it was neither in Pottinger's Road nor in Portugal Street, and yet was in both. The window which looked on to the road contained the groceries; scuttles full of tea, and boxes of brown and lump and granulated sugar, and sometimes, about Christmas, large pieces of preserved peel. The window which looked into Portugal Street was less interesting; it contained provisions—bacon and ham and eggs and tins of corned beef. But even these were more entertaining than hardware and paraffin oil. Behind the shop were the store-rooms, full of corn-bins and bales and boxes. At one time Mr. Peden had lived over his shop, but the increase of his business had brought him an increase of pride and caused him to remove his family to a villa beyond "the Arches" in what was vaguely called "the country," and now the

upper rooms of the house were used as stores. Bags
of flour and meal and bran filled what formerly was
the drawing-room! An enchanting shop, Mr. Peden's,
recalling the ends of the earth to Robert. Sam Peden
would let him thrust the white scoop into the flour or
bury his hands deep in the corn-bins or lift tea in a
copper-coloured scoop from the stencilled wooden
boxes in which it had been brought from India and
China and Ceylon. There were pictures of tea-planta-
tions on some of the boxes. Indian girls with big, dark
eyes daintily gathered the tea-leaves or paced along
sunlit roads with jars of water poised on their dusky
heads! . . . There was nothing in his mother's shop
to remind him of the wild and wasteful places of the
world, but he could hardly turn round in Mr. Peden's
shop without seeing something which had come from
the hands of brown or black or yellow men.

There was romance, too, in Mr. Scarlett's shop, a
smaller and less rambling one than Mr. Peden's. It
also had two windows, but both of them looked on to
Pottinger's Road. All that Mr. Scarlett had in Modesty Row, which was at his end of the Terrace, was a
blank wall, broken only by his side-door, on which
infuriated theologians scrawled insults to the Pope and
sometimes indecencies which sent Mr. Scarlett trembling to his scullery for a bucket of water. The chief
glory of Mr. Scarlett's windows was a coloured play-
bill of the piece being performed at the Theatre Royal.
He received, so it was said, at regular intervals a free
pass for two persons to the upper circle for exhibiting
the play-bills, and Robert, when he discovered this,
once waylaid the bill man and induced him to part
with a poster. But Mrs. Dunwoody refused to exhibit

it in her window. "There's enough tomfoolery in the world already, without me adding to it," she said, thrusting the bill into the fire. "But you'll get a free pass for some of the plays," Robert said to tempt her. "Aye," he retorted, "for the ones nobody'll go to!"

Mr. Scarlett sold tobacco and pipes, and his windows were full of tobacco in bars and flakes and shreds, yellow and brown and black, to smoke and to chew. There were clay pipes and briar pipes and pipes made of meerschaum, with amber ends. Robert loved the yellow, shredded tobacco, called "Honeydew," but more for its name than for itself. His chief pleasure was in the black jars of loose tobacco, and Tom Logan, who was Mr. Scarlett's apprentice, would sometimes take down a jar and let him snuff up the smell. He would show him big, brown leaves of tobacco, like long withered docks, and pictures of plantations in Cuba, and tell him strange and incredible stories of cigars which cost as much as half a crown apiece. Kings and millionaires would smoke away a labourer's wages for a whole week in a single night! They would toss one-and-three-penceworth of cigar into the gutter with as little concern as Robert would show in tossing away an apple-core. That was magnificent and splendid extravagance to think about! Mrs. Dunwoody could not contain herself when he reported those legends of waste to her. "God'll make them rue it on the Last Day," she said in her horror. "D'you not think He wastes a bit Himself?" Robert innocently asked. Her eyes gaped as she listened to him. "Is that the way you speak of the Almighty God?" she demanded, slapping his face.

III

He did not go so often to Mr. Scarlett's shop—
though Tom Logan was a born romancer—as he went
to Mr. Peden's. There was a bogey-woman in it. Mr.
Scarlett was a bachelor, possessed of an aged, bed-rid-
den, but determined mother who would not permit him
to marry, nor did he dare to disobey her until she was
dead and deeply buried in the city Graveyard. Only
once did Robert see her, but the memory abided in his
mind for the whole of his life. One Fair day, a
bewildered bull, on its way to the market, ran amok
and plunged headlong into Mr. Scarlett's shop, almost
wrecking it. Mr. Scarlett was not an agile man, but he
took a flying leap across his counter, and landed on
Tom Logan who was lying on the floor. There was a
swirl of smashed pipes and broken glass and heaving
tobacco, out of which a lashing tail protruded, while
the drovers, who were drunk, made unavailing noises
of persuasion. One of them, a man with moist, drink-
sodden eyes, coaxed the bull with incessant repetitions
of, "Ah, come on, now, come on, like a good bull!"
but, except that it lashed his face with its tail, it
ignored him. Mr. Scarlett, realising that he was pro-
tected by the counter, rose from Tom Logan's chest and
ordered the drover to take his bull out of that.

"This is no place for it," he said, a little impotently,
adding that some one would have to pay for the dam-
age that had been done.

The bull pawed the floor of the shop and then bel-
lowed horribly. It thrust its horns into a large tobacco
cabinet, dragging it with a clatter of broken glass to
the ground, and then turned to gaze on Mr. Scarlett,

who wavered away from the counter, treading on Tom Logan's hand as he did so. "Take it away out of that!" he shouted.

"I will, sir, if you'll tell me how," said the drover, whom disaster had not sobered.

"It's not my business to tell you! . . ."

Another crash as the bull swept a great tray of pipes on to the floor. One of the constables in the crowd proposed to the sergeant of police that he should send for a rifle to shoot the beast, but before the sergeant could make up his mind whether to accept the suggestion or rebuke the proposer of it, Mr. Scarlett's kitchen-door was opened, and old Mrs. Scarlett, "looking like the Day of Judgment," appeared. She had a soiled nightcap on her crumpled gray hair, and a faded plaid shawl over her nightdress. She stood unsteadily for a few moments against the lintels of the door while she surveyed the scene, and then her blazing eyes met her son's. "You shouldn't be up, ma!" he began, but she turned impatiently away from him, and regarded the bull. "Shoosh on out of that!" she said, waving her gnarled hands at it. And amazingly the bull ceased to lash its tail, and allowed itself to be led away. Robert ran across the street as fast as his legs would carry him, and stood just inside the shop-door. He saw Mr. Scarlett shamefacedly come from behind the counter and try to meet his mother's eyes with some valour. He saw Mr. Scarlett's glance quaver and finally fall.

"You great gumph you!" the old woman said to her son. "You great, big gumph! And you that's afeard of a bull want to marry a wife! God pity you, you daft, demented man you!"

She went back to her bed, nor did she leave it again

until she was carried to the burial-ground. Robert saw her coffin being lowered from the upstairs window to the street—the stairs were too narrow and twisted for it to be brought down by them—and he thought to himself that she was being obstinate to the end, giving as much trouble as she could even on her way to her grave. Almost he expected her to sit up in her shroud and ask the funeral men if they thought that was any way to bury a decent woman!

The thought of her, while she lived, lying upstairs in the front room, grim and gray and able to subdue mad bulls, frightened Robert, and when he went to hear Tom Logan's romances and to fill his fists with shredded tobacco and snuff up the smell of it, he did so with some apprehension lest the kitchen-door should suddenly swing open, and the terrible old woman come and shoosh him away! He had made up his mind about her; she was a witch; and he had read and heard too much about witches and their ways to care greatly for their company.

IV

These were the shops that enthralled him. Another one, two terraces along Pottinger's Road, owned by Mr. Corcoran, the butcher and flesher, had some interest for him, too, but more on account of Mr. Corcoran's claim to be a purveyor of meat to the military than on account of his shop or its contents. Mr. Corcoran was a widower, and careless in his habits—his servant-girls nearly always had children by him—and there was a sound suspicion that the room behind his shop was dirty and neglected. Yet marvellously he announced to the neighbourhood in curly, golden letters on his sign-board that he fed the troops. No one had ever seen the military buying meat from him, nor were any of the garrisons near his house, but he got advantage and reputation from the announcement, which, Mrs. Dunwoody said, might well be true, since he was more likely to visit the military with his meat than they were to visit him in search of it. Robert's respect for Mr. Corcoran was increased when he proposed to his mother, after a visit to Linden's tea-shop, that she should follow Linden's example and put the Royal Arms above the window. She told him that any one who did that without a warrant signed by the Queen's authority would be put in prison—and God alone knew when he would be let out again! Thereafter, he imagined Mr. Corcoran receiving copious correspondence from royalties and exalted generals, commanding him to supply them with a nice joint of beef or perhaps a plateful of chops. It was known to the world that Queen Victoria had a healthy appetite, God bless her, and why shouldn't she, and her with all the trouble of governing the country, and that she ate a chop every night of her life before going to bed. The labour of serving her alone, Robert realised, was hard, but when one added to it the feeding of her sons and their families and her regiments of soldiers, it was clear that Mr. Corcoran had his work cut out for him. Sometimes an immense pile of speckled sausages would lie on a large china plate in Mr. Corcoran's open window, and Robert, regarding them with awe and admiration, would say to Brenda Cairnduff or to himself, if he were alone, "Them's for the soldiers or mebbe the queen's family!" Once, when he had money, Brenda had dared him to go into the shop and offer to buy some of them, and he,

declining to be daunted by her, went in and rapped
on the counter until Mr. Corcoran, looking sleepy-eyed,
came into the shop.

"I want a half-pound of them sausages," he said,
expecting to be arrested or ordered out of the shop.

Mr. C———————————gh sausages to weigh
———————————————hem in newspaper.
———————————————gn that he had sold
———————————————non boy.
———————————————by his experience.
———————————————id to Brenda.
———————————————queen at all," she

———————————————n?" he repeated.
———————————————e said.

But the glamour of Mr. Corcoran's reputation sur-
vived that test, and Robert would watch him departing
each morning in his light cart, which was rarely washed
and always needed a coat of paint, and wonder to himself what bloody sights the butcher and flesher would
see before the day was done. The slaughtering of
cattle, for certain, but that was part of his occupation
and hardly sufficient by itself to excite awe and wonder.
He might, and this was Robert's darling hope, see
fierce fighting in the soldiers' camps. He imagined that
the training of recruits included the slaying of real
people, so that the soldiers should not feel uncomfort-
able about killing when they went to a war. He had
cause for this belief. John Kernaghan, who drove an
outside car, had spent a short time in the militia, and
had sworn, when spoken to about it, that he had been
in the habit of shooting and stabbing and generally
slaughtering as many as seven people a day during

his training at the Kinnegar, and that once the militia's manœuvres had been seriously hampered through a sudden shortage of killable people. Now Robert knew why the barracks were nearly always in Catholic neighbourhoods. The soldiers would naturally prefer to practise their killing on Papists than on good Protestants. For what other reason could their barracks be so convenient to the Catholic cemetery? Remembering what John Kernaghan had told him, Robert daily saw Mr. Corcoran depart on his rounds, and in his fancy followed him. He would be delivering a roast of meat to the colonel's wife, and while she was paying for it, he might see a couple of Catholics stabbed to death with bayonets or shot to pieces from a cannon. He had seen a picture once of executions in India. Sepoys were tied to the mouths of cannons! . . . Was it any wonder that a man accustomed to such sights as these in the course of his day's work sometimes forgot to wash himself and rarely remembered to wash his cart, and was unparticular about servant-girls?

Once, stealing into Mr. Corcoran's stable in the evening, he examined the cart-wheels to see if they were stained with blood; but there were no stains, and Robert acknowledged that even if there had been they might have been from the blood of cattle and not from the blood of Catholics.

V

He had many and singular thoughts about Catholics, who had the fascination of mysterious and forbidden people for him. Sometimes he peered through the windows of repositories at the crucifixes and scapulars and rosaries and statues of saints and Holy Families and, most of all, the pictures of the Sacred Heart. These last oddly repelled him, though he could not have said why. There was Jesus, in a blue and red robe, pointing to a hole in His side, where a large and very regular heart was visible. Flames rose from it, and a wreath of thorns encircled its head. Great gouts of blood dropped from it, and a cross stood up from the flames! . . . There were similar pictures of the Virgin, whose Heart, sometimes, was pierced with swords. Robert, horribly fascinated by them, gazed at the pictures and felt sick. They made him remember the one-armed man who sat in the gutter of the Queen's Bridge and exposed his mutilation to the gaze of the charitable. Always, when he had approached this man, Robert had resolved to shut his eyes, but they could not close, and when he came abreast of the beggar, he felt himself, half-horrified, half-fascinated, gazing on the stump! The Holy pictures filled him with disgust, yet he was compelled to look at them. Trembling and awe-stricken, he would creep to the chapel-door and peep in at the symbols of idolatry. He was astonished to find himself enthralled by the clusters of candles at the Virgin't feet and the flickering red light burning before the altar. Once, when he saw the High Altar itself richly lit up, he went right into the chapel and, lest he should be discovered to be a Protestant prowling about in a Catholic church, he dipped his fingers in the holy-water stoup, and made the sign of the Cross and genuflected to the Host, as he had seen a woman do. He slipped into a seat, and became frightened when he found that he was kneeling near a confessional in which a priest was sitting. Supposing

the priests were to force him to confess his sins! . . .
He hurried out of the chapel again, not daring to look
behind him, but even in the street, surrounded by good
Protestants, he could not forget the fascination of the
lit candles at the Virgin's feet or the lovely light they
made in the dusky chapel.

He knew the names of all the priests at St. Matthew's
and could have told the name of the Catholic Bishop
of the diocese when he did not know the name of the
Episcopal Bishop. Nevertheless, despite the fascination
of Catholicism for him, he had the queerest thoughts
about Catholics. He believed them to be an inferior
people. Unskilled labourers and servant-girls and publicans were Catholics; rich and respectable people were
nearly always Protestants. That surely was sufficient
proof for any one who had judgment. So certain was
he of the general disreputability of Catholics that one
day he charged Paddy Kane, for whom he had affection,
with the crucifixion of Christ.

"We didn't," Paddy passionately protested.

"Ah, but you did," Robert replied. "The Bible says
He was condemned and crucified by the Romans.
You're a Roman! . . ."

Paddy, who was slow in his thoughts, had no answer
ready for that, nor did he know how to retort when
Robert discovered in the Catholic use of crucifixes a
piece of shameless boasting, as if a Papist carried a
Cross solely that he might be able to say, "Yes, we did
that!"

"It's not true, I tell you," Paddy cried. "We
don't——"

"Then why do you have crucifixes?" Robert
demanded.

"It's—it's in memory of Him—to mind us about Him!"

"*We* don't have crucifixes, but we mind Him well enough!"

Then, because Paddy began to cry, Robert ceased to taunt him.

"Even if you are a Cathlik," he said, "I like you better'n anybody else!"

"All the same, it wasn't us that done it," Paddy insisted.

"Well, if you're sorry for it, that's all right," said Robert.

Brenda, listening in raptures to his argument with Paddy, sidled up to him and held his hand. 'You're an awfully good arguer," she murmured.

"Am I?" he said, drawing his hand away.

"Paddy can't argue at all——"

"You lave Paddy alone," he shouted at her, so that she blushed with vexation. He turned to Paddy. "Come on," he said. "Come on home with me, an' mebbe my ma'll give us our tay together!"

Brenda hesitated for a second. Then she said, "Let me come, too, Darkie?"

"No," he replied. "I don't want you. Standin' there, makin' little of Paddy!"

"You made little of him yourself."

"I didn't. I just toul' him what I thought of the Cathliks. I wouldn't make little of him. Would I, Paddy?"

"No," said Paddy. "But you shouldn't make little of my religion."

"Well, I won't any more. Come on!"

Nevertheless, his thoughts about Catholics continued

to be odd, and it did not appear to him incredible or wrong that they should be used by soldiers for bayonet-practice, though he cried terribly when he reflected that Paddy might some day be destroyed by a militiaman.

VI

Mrs. Dunwoody's shop was, undoubtedly, the dullest that Robert knew, but there were times when even it was enthralling to him. For two weeks in the year, at the Twelfth of July and at Christmas, the hardware shop became interesting and romantic. In July, the window and the greater part of the shop were filled with toy drums and paper Orange sashes. All the Protestant boys and many of the Protestant girls, if they were not to be suspected of poverty or infidelity to their faith, had to be provided with drums and sashes for the Twelfth, and Robert's recollection of the festival was for ever associated with masses of drums and piles of paper sashes. There were big drums and little drums —drums that a boy of fourteen could thump without smashing the skins, and drums that a baby, still sucking its comforter, could manage to hold and to beat. Robert never had any wish to own a drum, for mere banging and noise seemed poor entertainment to him, but he loved to watch the stock of drums steadily being diminished as the Twelfth drew near. The eleventh night was the great night, for then the last and most vigorous rush for drums was made. He would stand outside the shop, looking into the window where the drums were piled in columns that reached from the floor to the ceiling, and wait for them to disappear. First, his mother and his elder brother, Alec, would

work their way through the stock in the shop. Then,
the shop depleted, would come the thrilling moment
when Alec would mount the step-ladder and take down
the first drum from the nearest pile in the window, and
then the next and the next, until there were no more
drums left. The shop remained open very late on the
eleventh night, and Robert was allowed to stay out of
bed long after his time for retiring because there was
no one free to look after him. Up the road, men were
erecting an orange arch, made of dyed shavings, sling-
ing it from Jimmy Cæsar's chimney to the chimney on
McBratney's shop, but even this excitement did not
serve to allure him for long from the thrilling window.
His heart would beat faster as he saw the last column of
drums dwindling. Would the final drum of all be
sold? Would the window be emptied? He loved to
see it stripped bare, and would say to himself when it
was, "There, that lot's done with! Nothing's left.
We can start all over again, with everything fresh and
new!" If the last drum should remain unsold, his
mother would give it to him, but he never wished it to
remain unsold so that he might have it. Ardently he
desired it to be bought. Had no purchaser appeared,
and he had had the money, he would have bribed a boy
to buy it so that he might not be cheated out of his
pleasure in the depleted window. . . . When, at last
and very late, all the drums and sashes were sold, he
would go into the shop and find his mother and Alec
sitting behind the counter, worn out. The cash-drawer
would be drawn from its socket so that Mrs. Dunwoody
might more comfortably count and separate the coins;
the pennies and sixpences and rarer half-crowns. Now
and then, a dirty pound note would be taken from a

little recess at the back of the drawer. When all the coins had been counted, the pennies stacked into columns of a shilling each, the shillings into columns of a pound, Mrs. Dunwoody would announce the grand total. This was her privilege and was not to be usurped by any one. Alec, having helped with the counting and casting, already knew what the total was, but he was aware of his duty and affected not to know it. He leant forward almost as eagerly as Robert, to hear his mother's announcement. "Two shillings more than last Twelfth!" she would add, when she had stated the total, or, "Three-and-sixpence less this year than last!" The heap of coins meant little to Robert as money, but much as excitement. He would look at his mother's fingers, cut, sometimes, through too hasty handling of the drums, and take pride in them; honourable wounds sustained in the great effort to empty the window. When he went to bed, he dreamt of mountains of drums being torn down by his mother and Alec while mountains of pennies and shillings rose up in their place.

There was greater excitement at Christmas, for then the window was decorated with frosted holly and cotton wool, and there was a large, mechanical toy performing in the centre of the Christmas goods. Mrs. Dunwoody thought carefully and for a long while about each year's mechanical toy. It had to be different from its predecessor and more unusual than any other toy in the road. Early in November, Robert began to wonder what surprise she would spring on her customers at Christmas, but he did not dare to ask her for a hint of it, partly because he himself was anxious to be astonished, but chiefly because he was afraid to. Once,

in his excitement, he had given away the secret of the
coming toy to the daughter of one of his mother's rivals,
and her carefully-planned surprise had been ruined
because her rival had bought an exactly similar toy
and exhibited it to the public two days before hers was
due to be displayed. There was no toy at all in her
window that year, and Robert's remorse caused him to
hold his tongue about novelties ever after. At Christmas, as at the Twelfth, he loved to see the window
being emptied until at last there was left only the
mechanical toy, still performing its tricks as if the window were full. He then went happily to bed, hanging
his stocking on the post with as much expectation as if
he did not know exactly what would be in it on Christmas morning. There would be some pennies and a
shilling—the latter of no earthly use to him since it was
immediately buried in the Post Office Savings Bank—
and an apple and an orange and some sweets. A book
would be tied to the bed-rail. Down at the bottom
of the stocking, stretching from heel to toe, would be a
toy pistol and some paper caps to fire in it. The pistol
appeared in the stocking each year, but Robert felt no
resentment over that. Immediately he was awake, he
would open the stocking, seize the pistol and, having
loaded it with one of the paper caps, would fire it close
to Alec's ear. His brother, tired by his work, would
leap up with a start, exclaiming, "My God Almighty,
what's happened!" and then, seeing Robert laughing
beside him, would add, "I'll cut the legs off you, dis-
turbin' me like that!" and lie down again. Robert
always laughed to himself for a long time after Alec
had fallen asleep. "I scared him again," he would
whisper to the bedclothes. "I scared the wits out of

him. He near jumped out of his skin with the fright I gave him!" But scaring Alec was easy.

VII

At the back of the Terrace was a hall which had formerly been Mr. Peden's stable, but was now a Salvation Army "barracks." Its shape was so irregular that it could not be described. It bellied out in the centre, and had a platform at one end, low in front and high behind. The penitent-form was immediately in front of the platform, and here the saved and repentant sinners knelt in an agony of remorse and offered themselves for redemption. The "barracks" had a thin roof, made of tarred felt stretched across light rafters. It was a leaky roof, and on wet nights the rain dribbled through the felt and splashed on the floor below. In the winter, when the stove was alight, drops of rain would sometimes fall on the hot lid and make a loud sizzling sound until they had evaporated. Very rarely did the officer in command fail to illustrate the tortures of the damned by the raindrops on the stove. "That's how you'll sizzle in hell if you don't get right with God!" Nevertheless, the gospel of the Army was a cheerful one, and there was more singing than moaning in the meetings, and the soldiers laughed oftener than they groaned. A narrow entry separated the houses in the Terrace from the Army "barracks," and Robert was able now and then to steal out of his mother's back door and climb up a low wall which led to the roof of the "barracks." He would scramble close to the sloping window, pulled open by cords, and listen to the meeting. This was a better way of listening than sitting in the hall itself, but he had to be careful not to be seen, for his mother had forbidden him to climb on to the roof. He liked the Army meetings better than the Presbyterian service which he was compelled to attend every Sunday morning. The Army had officers and soldiers in uniform—blue tunics and bright red jerseys, emblazoned with the burning sign of Blood and Fire. The worshippers were not called a congregation; they were called a corps. They had a band and a brilliant flag, and the women soldiers carried jingling tambourines. Some of the young soldiers were being taught to play the flute! . . .

The singing was hearty and abundant, with hymns set sometimes to music-hall tunes that were jolly to listen to. Even when the hymn was mournful, it was heartily mournful. The band would play with all its force; the tambourines would be jingled in some sort of harmony; and those of the soldiers who were not in the band and had no tambourines would clap their hands together while they sang. A jolly religion! There were meetings every night, and three meetings on Sunday. Mrs. Dunwoody sometimes went to the Army meetings on week-nights, but never on the Sabbath when her own church, she said, demanded her presence, but she liked to see Robert going to them, despite his deplorable custom of getting "saved" during specially interesting meetings. "I'm glad you're saved, son," she said to him once when he had returned to her from the penitent-form, "but there's no need to do it so often. God knows all about you, and He'll mebbe think it disrespectful of you if you make a habit of it!" He did not dare to tell her on that occasion that he had got "saved" simply for effect. An old man had stum-

bled to the penitent-form, leaving a gap between him
and the next person who had "given himself to Jesus."
That was the only vacant place at the penitent-form,
and suddenly Robert thought that if he were to fill it,
the captain, perceiving the old man and the young boy
kneeling side by side, would exclaim dramatically, "God
has room for everybody, the young and the old. Look,
brothers and sisters, at this young child and this old
man begging for mercy at His holy feet! . . ." Tears
filled his eyes as he pictured the scene and he rose up
and went to the penitent-form and knelt down by the
old sinner's side. He covered his face with his hands
and sobbed aloud. There was intense emotion in the
meeting, and Robert was overcome by it, but he did not
forget to listen for the words which he was sure would
soon be said—and presently the captain said them! His
certainty that they would be spoken convinced him of
God's presence. Who else but God could have put
into his head the idea of getting "saved" at that moment
or have made him feel so certain that the captain would
publicly refer to his conversion? He knew that the
angels were flying through the heavens, singing halle-
lulias of joy over his salvation. The hosts of Heaven
were specially observing this one out of all the redeemed
sinners of the world! . . . Nor was his pride reduced
when one of the soldiers coming to wrestle with his
soul, recognised him as the inveterate penitent, and said
in disgust, "Och, it's you again, is it?" and passed on
to the next sinner. What did it matter to him that the
saving soldier disbelieved in his redemption? Had it
not worked out as he had anticipated? Was he not
exalted by it? He returned to his mother, uplifted and
full of glory. . . .

But more than the meetings, he loved listening to

them from the roof, and would long have continued to listen to them from that perilous perch had it not been for the night of disaster. On a Sunday night, when Mrs. Dunwoody and Alec were at church together, and he was left at home with his sisters, Mattie and Margaret, he waited until they were busy with books and stole out of the back door into the entry and climbed on to the Army roof, where he lay at his length, listening to the singing and the tambourines and the beating of the drums until the supreme moment when the testimonies were given and the saved sinners declared what wicked acts they had done before their conversion. Paddy Gallagher, a genial, kindly soul, had been in the habit, so he said, of throwing his wife out of an upstairs window every Saturday night until God got a grip of him, praise His Holy Name, and brought him to his knees. Never once since that happy day had he thrown Mrs. Gallagher out of the window. And what God had done for him, He could do for the worst of them! . . . When the testimonies had been delivered, the captain began an emotional address in which he described the bliss of the saved and the misery of the damned. Then the soldiers of the platform descended upon the unsaved in the body of the "barracks" and urged them to come to God. The captain, in a crooning voice, started a hymn:—

> You'll see the Great White Throne
> And stand before it all alone,
> Waiting for the Judge to call
> When the stars begin to fall.

The saved and the unsaved sang the chorus:—

> My God, what a morning, morning, morning,
> My God, what a morning when the stars begin to fall.

The hall was packed with unregenerate men and women, and Captain Clifford, an appealing preacher, felt waves of emotion pouring through him. This was to be the greatest night in that corps. The Holy Ghost was present—he was certain of the Spirit's presence, and he became more and more fervent in his appeals, so that the unsaved were intensely stirred. Robert, lying on the roof, could hear him counting the converts as they streamed to the penitent-form, and, peering through the window, saw that there was a double row of sinners already offered for redemption.

"Hallelulia! Another soul for Jesus! That makes fifteen for God; Five more'll make twenty, and a heavy defeat for the Devil! Five more for glory. Who'll be the first candidate for heaven? God offers you a free pass to everlasting joy! Oh, there's grace abounding here this night. I can feel God groping for His own! . . . Ah, here comes another! And another! Glory be to God! Glory be to God! . . ."

Robert, hauling himself closer to the window, saw a man reeling up the hall, and heard him shouting, "I'm a Cathlik, but, dammit, I'll get saved, too!" Captain Clifford asssured the sinner that God was not particular. "Catholics or Protestants, it's all one to Him. He can save anybody or anything. Come unto Me, all ye that labour and are heavy-laden, and I will give ye rest. That doesn't just mean Catholics or Protestants. It means the whole wide world; brown, black, red, white, and yellow! . . ." With that, the Catholic was hauled out of hell into heaven. The hymn was started again. "My God, what a morning, morning, morning, my God, what a morning when the stars begin to fall." Suddenly, there was a commotion in the middle of the hall; a drunkard was seized with delirium tremens.

He stood up in his seat, pale and perspiring, and yelled
with fear. The devil was after him. The devil had got
a hold of him and was hauling him down to hell. He
wanted to be saved, but the devil would not let him
be saved. Wouldn't the captain come and help to
rescue him from hell? . . . There was a tremendous
stir in the hall, and Captain Clifford, feeling that this
was a task for him and not for the rank and file,
descended from the platform so that he might wrestle
with the Evil One for the man's soul. Robert, straining
at the window, could just see the sinner in the crowd
of soldiers who were begging him to come to Jesus.
They closed in on him, led by their captain, and shut
him out from Robert's view, but not from his hearing.
The unhappy drunkard was piteously asserting that he
did not want to go to hell, and Robert, now persuaded
that the devil was clawing at him and dragging him
out of the arms of God and Captain Clifford, carelessly
shifted himself on the tarred felt so that he might better
behold the fearful and enthralling sight. He was so
intent on seeing the devil that he did not hear the felt
sagging and ripping beneath him. It parted, and with
a shriek he fell through the roof into the middle of the
throng of excited saints and sinners. A yell of terror
burst from the delirious drunkard as Robert's body
landed at his feet, and he rose up, foaming at the
mouth, and flung himself almost in a single bound on
the penitent-form with prayers for pity that nearly rent
the heavens as Robert had rent the roof! . . .

VIII

When Robert had recovered from his bruises and his
fright, his mother solemnly beat him with the tawse.

Captain Clifford's plea that he should be forgiven because he had been an instrument for good was disregarded by her. Undoubtedly Robert had precipitated the drunkard into the arms of Jesus, but he had done so unintentionally. Times without number, she had forbidden him to climb on to the Army roof. It was bad enough for him to climb on to an ordinary roof, but to climb there, "peeping at God like that!" was unforgivable, even when, as on this occasion, God had used him to pluck a brand from the burning. So she beat him with the leather tawse. But he did not complain or care. The strokes on his bare pelt were painful, but he did not shed a tear. The drunkard had miraculously recovered from his delirium and was now a saved, if shaken, man; and Robert had been the instrument chosen by God Himself to perform this miracle. Almost he rejoiced in his beating, and when his mother, suddenly anxious for him, said, "Am I hurting you, chile dear?" he proudly replied, "Yes, ma, but I'm not mindin' it!" Immediately she threw down the leather tawse and hugged him. "I know what I'll do with you," she said, "I'll make a minister of you!" Then, as suddenly as she had hugged him, she thrust him from her. "Kneel down," she said, "and ask God to keep you from feelin' too proud of yourself!" He knelt down, as she bade him, and repeated the words which she dictated, that he might be delivered from spiritual pride and grow up, humbly and meekly, to serve the Lord. But there was no power in his petition, for he was full of pride.

THE SECOND CHAPTER

I

PEOPLE said of Mrs. Dunwoody that she was a masterful woman. "She's entitled to anybody's respect." Sometimes, when she looked up from her ledger and surveyed her shop, a thrill of pride would run through her body. She had created a thriving business without the help of any man. Her manners and her thoughts were modest, but she could not refrain from boasting to herself—for she would not boast to any one else—when she remembered that she had reared four young children, suddenly bereft of their father who had been drowned with his crew in the Eastern Pacific, and had founded and maintained this flourishing shop. More than once she had nearly been daunted, but she had kept her courage and now her reward was sure and ample. Her eldest son, Alec, was a sober and civil and industrious lad, coming up to twenty, amenable to her bidding and ready to take the heaviest part of her work. The two girls, Mattie and Margaret, were well enough. Mattie, the elder and a year younger than Alec, was the pretty one of the family, and aware of it, too. She was not so amenable to her mother as Alec was, but she was amenable enough for a good-looking girl. A suspicion occasionally crossed Mrs. Dunwoody's mind that she would have trouble with Mattie, who had a stiff

temper that was rarely shown and hard to conquer. But
Mattie, on the whole, was manageable. So, too, was
Margaret, now seventeen and plain like Mrs. Dunwoody herself; a pale, thin-featured girl, with light blue
eyes and a quick, running sort of laugh that people
liked. Her temper was as quick as her laugh, and she
had a great deal to say for herself and often merited
her mother's rebuke: "You have as many opinions as
would sink a ship!" She read books. Twice every
week she walked across the bridge and along the Sand
Quay to the Free Library in the centre of the city where
she borrowed a novel that might be good, but was more
likely to be daring. There was one story she had
brought home, called *The Sorrows of Satan!* . . . Mrs.
Dunwoody had sternly bidden Margaret to take the
dreadful book back again, and had thought, for awhile,
of sending a letter to the Lord Mayor and Corporation
to ask them if they realised on what sort of literature
the rates were being squandered. When she was Margaret's age and had bothered to read anything, she had
read *Only a Chestnut Burr* and *Jessica's First Prayer*
and *The Lamplighter* and *Christy's Old Organ*—good
religious stories, well larded with texts and improving
sentiments. Margaret yawned over *Christy's Old
Organ,* but yawn as she might she would not be allowed
to bring books like *The Sorrows of Satan* into the house!
. . . Mrs. Dunwoody did not discover until some
months had elapsed that Margaret had concealed the
shameful story in her bedroom and had read it there
while her mother was busy in the shop. She had even
read parts of it aloud to Mattie, and Mattie, so amenable to authority, had shamelessly listened! . . . A
difficult girl, Margaret, but Mrs. Dunwoody did not

expect to have serious trouble with her. She would be a poor sort of a mother, she said to herself, if she could not handle a daughter or two.

It was Robert, her youngest child, three years younger than Margaret, who deeply troubled her thoughts. He was her dearest child, her heart's darling, born after his father's drowning, and she had put her pride in him. Alec's career was plain enough; a good, careful, obedient son who would carry on her business for her and ensure the comfort of her old age. Mattie and Margaret would marry sensible, well-set-up and prospering men of her own choice, and would live near her so that she might easily and often see her grandchildren. These three were to be solid members of her family, contenting themselves with keeping what she had made as safe and as sound as she had made it. But Robert was destined to do more than this for her; he was to exalt her name and restore pride to her family. The boy had brains, and if only he would consent to use them well! . . . She rubbed her chin with a forefinger. Would he use them well? There was a wild and wayward strain in him that filled her with dismay and apprehension. The schoolmaster said that Robert could learn well enough when he tried, but that he seldom tried. "He hasn't the patience, Mrs. Dunwoody. His mind's never on what he's doing, and if you ask him what it *is* on, he doesn't know. He's the fearfullest wee fellow for letting his imagination wander. When he's in the mood for learning, nobody can beat him——!"

"Can't you keep him in the mood?" she interrupted, feeling that this should be easy work for a schoolmaster, armed as he was with authority and a rod.

"Can you keep water from running through your fingers?" Mr. Gebbie replied.

"No," she answered, "but Robert's not water."

"I'm not so sure about that. Anyway, whatever he learns, he'll learn for himself in his own way. I can give a good guess at what'll happen to the majority of the children that goes through my hands, Mrs. Dunwoody, for indeed, we're near all of a pattern, but I wouldn't take the risk of guessing about Robert."

"D'you think he'd make a minister?"

"He might. But then, he might not. Whatever he does, he'll be a bit disconcerting——!"

II

The talk with Mr. Gebbie made Mrs. Dunwoody uneasy. She loved authority, and she had an excessive pride in her family which made her wish to keep her children about her even when, in due time, they should marry. Her reading rarely went beyond the *Evening Telegraph* and the Old Testament. As she turned over the pages of the big Bible, bound and clasped in brass, and read about the prolific Jews who were so unaccountably chosen to be God's people, she told herself that none of them had so much pride of family and desire for parental authority as she had. She would have enjoyed being a ruler in Israel. To sit before her tent in the evening time, with her children and her children's children and their flocks and herds circling around her, would have given her immeasurable joy. She rarely read the New Testament, but the Old was seldom from her thoughts. No one had ever heard her say how profoundly shocked she was when she read for

the first time Christ's reply to the announcement that
His mother and brethren waited outside. "Who is my
mother, or my brethren?" She could not have acknowledged that Christ's disregard of family life made her
prefer the Old Testament to the New, because she was
not aware of her preference, but it was a fact that she
felt happy with the latter only when she came upon the
genealogies. She loved the stories of the patriarchs
and got intense pleasure from reading aloud the long
list of "begats." The first chapter of the gospel according to St. Matthew thrilled her. She felt that it properly
belonged to the book of Genesis, that it was misplaced
in the New Testament. "Abraham begat Isaac; and
Isaac begat Jacob; and Jacob begat Judas and his brethren; and Judas begat Pharos and Zara of Thamar; and
Pharos begat Esrom, and Esrom begat Aram." She
almost licked the "begats" with her lips and tongue
as she slowly rolled them out of her mouth. "There's
family for you!" she would say. "There was great
quality and length of years in them people!" Margaret,
impatiently listening, once replied, "It's a queer thing
never to mention their mothers. Nobody but their oul'
das!"

"Wheesht, daughter dear," Mrs. Dunwoody commanded. "That's no way to talk of the Bible."

"All the same, Bible or no Bible," Margaret continued, undaunted, "I think they ought to say something
about their mothers and their daughters. You'd near
think them people come into the world without a
woman near the house."

Mrs. Dunwoody, who had secretly sympathised with
Margaret's opinion—was she not herself an example of
a woman who had reared and sustained a fine family?

—could not allow this freedom of speech to go unchecked. "You're ondacent, girl," she said, "and you can just go to your bed this minit and ask God's forgiveness."

"All the same——" Margaret began, but her mother would not listen to her. "Away wi' ye," she said, and Margaret, remembering a novel under her bed, went.

Mrs. Dunwoody sometimes let it be known that she was descended from a Downshire gentleman who owned land and let it to farmers, one of whom became her grandfather. Her grandmother had committed the mortal sin of marrying beneath her, and had been ignored by her father and his family ever afterwards. But although the De Lacys and their recognised descendants disdained to know Mrs. Dunwoody, if, indeed, they were aware of her existence, they could not keep their blood out of her veins, and she proudly exhibited to those who would look the signs of her good descent. When Robert spoke to her once of the eminence of Mr. Peden—eminent because his shop was bigger than hers and he lived in a detached villa in the country—she laughed and held out her fine, shapely hands and bade him observe what the hands of people of quality were like.

"Look at my lips," she said. "And my face. Can't you tell by my face?"

She made him aware of his own shapely hands, and told him that he had a look of breeding seen only in those who had "the quality" in them. "Mr. Peden's a nice, dacent man," she admitted, "but he hasn't the quality in him. His family's nothing. His grandfather was a clauber-man—not," she hurriedly added, "that I'm making little of him for that. I'm not. But there's

a queer differs atween them that's up and them that's
going up, and the differs is quality, son!"

Robert could not detect this difference, and his failure
distressed her. He said it was finer to be Mr. Peden,
rising from an ancestry of scavengers and street-sweep-
ers, than to be Mrs. Dunwoody, living on her unac-
knowledged descent from a landed gentleman. He
could not easily explain his belief to her, chiefly because
she was impatient about it, but he made her understand
that he was not deeply impressed by his distant rela-
tionship to the De Lacys and that he was immensely
impressed by the importance of Mr. Peden. Once, at a
public function in the Ulster Hall, he had seen the Mr.
De Lacy of that time, and had remained unstirred by
the spectacle. "I'd rather have Mr. Peden any day,"
he said. "Sure, thon's a dreepy-drippy sort of a man!
. . ."

None of her children shared her family pride, but
Robert's failure to share it distressed her more than the
failure of Alec or the girls. They were Dunwoodys, she
said to herself, with more of their father in them than
of her, and they must live like Dunwoodys, decent and
civil; but Robert was a De Lacy and must rise to the
De Lacey level. She closely watched him for signs of
"the quality" and strove, as best she could, to strip
him of Dunwoodyness. When she came upon him
studying maps and tracing rivers from their source to
the sea, she rebuked him for wasting his time, not
because she thought he was wasting it, but because she
found signs of his father in this map-reading and
wished to remove them. The thought that Robert
might follow his father to sea sent her shuddering to
her knees. . . . This wandering about the oceans of the

world filled her with fear and disgust. She had lost her
husband because he could not content himself in one
place, and she had no wish to lose her son. It was not
only the recollection of her drowned husband, whom
she had loved and by whom she had been loved, that
made her unwilling to think of Robert as a sailor. She
frequently announced her wish that people would "stay
in their own place." Half of her life had been spent in
Donaghreagh, where she was born, and the other half
in Belfast. Donaghreagh remained in her memory as a
dear affection, but her visits to it, after her removal to
Belfast, had been infrequent and widely separated from
each other. Travelling even so short a distance as that
was not to her taste. Death, indeed, was the chief cause
of her journeys, for she was punctilious about the duties
of the living to the dead, and she would take much
trouble to "pay respect" to some dead person whom
she had known in her youth, though possibly she had
not seen him or her for many years. A few times, she
had been persuaded to spend a day at Pickie or Ballyards, but these were all. She got no pleasure from
"trips"; she preferred to stay in her own place. So it
was that she rarely took journeys. Belfast is partly in
Antrim and partly in Down, but for her there was only
Down. She had never been in any part of Antrim
except that which was contained in Belfast, and
although she had heard of Portrush and Dublin and
London and New York and queer places with queer
names she had no wish to see them. "What would I
go trapesing there for?" she said when some one suggested that she should visit Dublin. "I know nobody
there." That was her conclusive retort to all sugges-
tions of travel. She knew nobody there. When Mr.

Peden went to the Ulster Convention in London during a Home Rule agitation, she surmised that the principal difference between London and Belfast was that London was bigger. "An' mebbe lonelier!" When Robert came running from Scarlett's shop, his head full of yarns spun for him by Tom Logan, or from Mr. Peden's to tell her of the wonders of China and Japan, she would listen without interest and chill his romance by saying, "Them places is all very well for the ones that have to live in them, but what would we be doin' there an' us not knowin' a soul?"

"But they're wonderful places, ma!" Robert insisted.

"Any place is wonderful if you don't live in it," she retorted. "I dare say the Chinamen think Belfast's the marvel of the world! Content yourself, son, in your own place, and don't go fillin' your mind with nonsensical nonsense. Everybody should stay where they're put, an' not go trampin' up and down the earth as if they couldn't rest anywhere."

That was her deepest conviction, that every one should stay in his own country with his own kin. If necessity compelled a man to leave the place where he was born, he should go where he was likely to find some of his friends. Mrs. Mercer's sons had emigrated, one after the other, until at last she, too, followed her eldest boy to Canada, where she died fretting for her home. Her second son had gone to the United States— "as far, seemingly, as he could get from his brother,"— one was in Australia, and the youngest was in South Africa. "It's strange them leavin' their own country," Mrs. Dunwoody remarked, "but it's stranger still them not all goin' thegether to the one country. You'd near think they wanted to separate their family." That any family should wish to disperse was a problem which she found hard to solve, but it was incredible to her that her own family should wish to disperse. When she forecast the future, she saw her life unfolding itself in her children, each of whom would be established in reputation and pride and prosperity by her side, with Robert as the brightest jewel in her crown. The name of the Dunwoodys would be famous in Ulster, and a day would come when the proud De Lacys would thankfully acknowledge them! Who knew but Robert would bring the Dunwoodys and the De Lacys into closer kindred by marrying the young De Lacy's daughter. . . .

III

Her business was increasing. Her cautious mind could no longer deny the increase or the unlikelihood that it might be converted into decline. Before long she would have to yield to Alec's suggestion that she should knock down the wall which separated the shop from the kitchen and double the size of the shop. The plan was already made, but she had been reluctant to act on it, because the kitchen had kindly memories for her. But Alec was right and wise. The wall must be pulled down. The return-room at the top of the first flight of stairs could be converted into a kitchen. When that was done, the whole of the ground-floor would be available for the sale of hardware, and her efforts to extend her trade would not be crippled by lack of room. She acknowledged to herself that the change ought to have been made a year or two before, but the loss of time did not seriously matter, for she had consolidated her trade and had not expended capital before she could safely do so. If the conversion were made now, the cost of it would be recovered before the time came when Robert must go to a more expensive school, and she would not then be hampered in her plans for him by lack of money. She called to Alec.

"Come here, son," she said.

He came from the street-door, and as she looked at him she thought how strange it was that Robert and he should be brothers. He had mild, gray eyes in which there was no sparkle—"like his Aunt Fanny's!" she said to herself—and his flat, white face had a flabby look, although it was not flabby. His faintly fair moustache seemed to be dribbling from his mouth, like weather-beaten tufts of gray grass, and when he spoke there was a fretful note in his voice that vaguely irritated his mother and caused her to tell herself that he was "an oul' Jenny-jo." Alec was extraordinarily submissive to his mother, desiring, or so it seemed, no will but hers, and almost girlishly eager to fulfil her wishes. Robert had none of his brother's submission to her authority. He seemed, sometimes, to be set on defying her. But Robert was her darling, and she found herself comparing the two boys always to the disadvantage of the elder. "If Alec was more like Robert, and Robert was more like Alec, I'd be the happy woman," she thought.

"Yes, ma," Alec said, standing before her.

Suddenly she felt impatient with him, observing for the first time that one side of his dribbling moustache was longer than the other. She wished he would have it properly trimmed and that he would remember his appearance. It did not seem right to her that one of her family should be careless of his looks. "But he's a good and amenable son," she said to herself, as if she were excusing him.

She described her plan to him.

"It would mebbe be better to open a branch shop," he said, "and leave this one alone."

"A branch! What put that notion into your mind?"

"I was thinkin' when you wouldn't pull the wall down before that mebbe you were right, an' we'd do better with a branch. Mattie an' you could manage this, an' I could look after the branch with a bit of help from Margaret on a Friday an' a Saturday."

"I had no notion of a branch," Mrs. Dunwoody said, dallying with the idea.

It was made clear to her that Alec had thought much about a branch, that the dearest dream of Alec's life now was that he might open a shop, subordinate to his mother's, but under his control. Mrs. Dunwoody thought for a few moments.

"No," she said decisively, "I don't like the idea—not yet awhile anyway. We'll enlarge this one first, an' then mebbe we'll think about a branch. We've a certain sure trade here, an' I don't want to take any risks for the present. You see, Alec, I have Robert's future to think about."

"It's just as you say, ma!" said Alec, unable to keep the note of disappointment out of his voice.

"You sound disappointed, Alec!" she exclaimed.

"Well, I am, ma, but of course I'll agree to whatever you say. I dare say you're right, too."

She considered. "I think I am," she replied, "but I'll not forget the idea. It's a good one. Had you any thought in your head where the branch might be?"

"Cromac Street," he answered.

She looked at him in astonishment, and then laughed. This was unusual decision in Alec. "You appear to have made up your mind about it all," she said. "I suppose you know the very shop you want? . . ."

"Yes, ma, I do. I've been askin' a wheen of questions from time to time, an' the man that has this shop isn't doin' well in it! . . ."

"That's no recommendation to me, Alec."

"It's his own fault. He drinks an' bets an' plays devil's cards, an' neglects his business."

"That's it, is it?"

"Aye. I think I could do well with it. The shop's in a very good position, with a lot of traffic passin' the door. The trams stop forenenst it."

"H'm! Well, I'll think about it. Keep your eyes open an' tell me what goes on. In the meantime, we'll have this wall down."

"Yes, ma."

They made plans and calculations, and then, irrelevantly, she said, "I suppose that man'll go bankrupt soon?"

He knew to whom she referred. "I should say he's near that already. Dacent enough sort of a man, but no control over himself. Always after this an' after that, an' never the same two minutes runnin'! . . ."

"Aye, indeed," Mrs. Dunwoody murmured.

"Just like Robert," said Alec.

She glanced at him sharply. "What's that you say?" she said.

"I said he was just like Robert. No stability."

"What makes you talk that way of your brother, an' him little more nor a child?" she angrily demanded.

"He has his nature for all that, ma, child or no child. You know rightly he's runnin' daft after one thing an' another, fillin' his head wi' talk——" There was terrible contempt in his tone when he said the word "talk." "You don't know the half about him I know. He's always talking to me about ships an' foreign countries an' adventures an' God alone knows what. Tom Logan is always crackin' on to him about travellin'— that's the latest notion—an' he's half astray in the head with the talk."

Mrs. Dunwoody did not immediately reply, and when she did, she spoke as if she were unconcerned. "Robert's right enough," she said. "Anyway, he's young yet."

"Mebbe," Alec answered, "but the kind of talk he's fond of 'll be no good til him in business or in the pulpit either, for that matter. It's sensible talk he needs, not *talk!*"

"Well, he'll be goin' to a bigger school soon, an' I dare say he'll amend his ways when he gets there."

"I hope so," said Alec in a tone that had no hope in it. "It's a pity he doesn't take more interest in the business. I wish he took the interest I do. Him an' me might run a branch or two atween us! . . ."

"I'm not thinkin' of puttin' Robert into business," his mother replied. "You know that well enough, Alec, an' there's no need for me to remind you of my intention."

At that moment, Robert came running from the street.

"Ma," he said to his mother, "would you believe the like of this? Tom Logan says there's places in the world where you dig a scoop in the water and bring up lumps of gold——!"

"Ah, wheesht with you," Mrs. Dunwoody angrily exclaimed. "That fellow Logan's demented."

IV

The conversion of the kitchen into the shop was quickly done, and while it was being made, Mrs. Dunwoody revolved Alec's plan for a branch shop in her mind. Her prestige would be considerably increased if she were the owner of two flourishing shops—and when she thought of this growth of reputation, she saw herself becoming the owner of many shops in each of which a member of her family would be manager. If she were to settle her children in comfortable circumstances, she need never fear to lose them from her side. Dunwoodys would be in every part of Belfast, all of them owing allegiance to her. Like Abraham, she might sit in the shade of the evening and consider her possessions and her children! In time, she would retire to a villa outside the city, and her children and their children would visit her. She imagined herself as an old woman in her garden in the summer nights, with her thriving descendants around her. Robert would often come to her, full of honour, and she would be proud of him. The others would be proud of him, too, and would feel no jealousy because she loved him more than she loved them. "My son, the minister," she would say, and people, knowing of his eminence, would pay respect to her! . . .

The sudden bankruptcy of the shopkeeper in Cromac Street sharply brought her to a decision, and the enlargement of the shop had hardly been completed when she agreed to instal Alec in the new one. His delight in it brought colour to his face. Mattie declared that he went to is as if he were going to the shore for a holiday and returned from it as healthy and happy as if he had enjoyed a month's sea-bathing.

"The walk over the two bridges does me a power of good," he said, but he knew that his happiness sprang from his possession of the shop. He worked hard so that his mother might not be fatigued by the changes in their life, and made Mattie and Margaret able to take complete charge of the old shop. "Just you take your rest," he said to his mother, "and leave us young ones to do the work. You've done your share! . . ."

She liked his solicitude for her, but did not submit to it. "No, no," she replied, "I've always had the direction of things, an' I'll keep it. I couldn't lie content if I didn't know where everything was."

"No doubt you're right, ma, but there's no needcessity for you to put yourself about. There's plenty of us to do the work. Robert's comin' up, too. Would you like to serve in the shop, Robert?"

"No, I would not," Robert replied.

Alec was affronted. "An' why not?" he demanded.

"I don't want to serve in it. That's why."

Mrs. Dunwoody smiled at her younger son. "It's a minister you want to be, son, isn't it?" she said.

"No, ma, I don't want to be that either."

She ceased to smile at him.

"Well, what do you want to be?" Alec shouted at him.

Robert paused for a moment, and then boldly said, "A sailor."

His mother flushed angrily. "Quit that talk," she said. "Quit that talk, do you hear me? Quit it, the pair of you. I've told you, Alec, more times nor I remember, that he's goin' to be a minister, so there's no needcessity for you or him to debate the matter atween you. An' you, Robert, be bid by me an' stop fillin' your head with romantical notions."

"I'd rather be a sailor nor anything," Robert insisted. "It's a quare fine life, a sailor's."

Her voice was raised as she replied, "What sort of a life, will you tell me? Home mebbe once in a blue moon, an' his childher hardly knowin' him. Mrs. McClurg in Spaniard Street has her children streamin' their eyes out every time her man comes home because they don't know who he is an' are 'feard of him. Two years an' more at a stretch he'll be away from her!"

"All the same, I want to go to sea," said Robert.

"You'll go to no sea. You'll stay here where your family is an' lead a dacent person's life. Sailor, indeed! The half of them drinkin' their way round the world, an' the other half drinkin' it back. The morra-morn I'll go an' see about gettin' you to a new school where they'll mebbe teach you sense an' not to talk so broad!"

He protruded his under lip. "I like talkin' broad. It's the way you talk. I like the way you talk."

She melted at once. "Yes, son, I know, but I want you to be better educated nor me."

He disregarded this. "I could get into the navy, ma," he said.

"The *what?*" The horror in her voice was indescribable.

"The navy. Me an' another lad got a paper at the post office about it. Here it is." He handed her the

pamphlet which glowingly described life in the navy.
She took it from him, glancing at it for a moment, and
then put it into the fire. "If I hear another word of
this," she said, "big as you are I'll skelp the life out
of you!"

He flushed at the threat of beating, for he was now
old enough to feel that punishment of that sort was
insulting. His cheeks darkened, and his eyes began to
burn with anger.

"Yous can all talk," he said, "till yous are blue in
the face, but I'm goin' to sea just as soon as ever I
can get."

"Och, away an' divert yourself," said Mrs. Dunwoody.

Alec did not speak.

On the following day, she arranged for Robert to
enter Martin's College. Later on, she said, he would
go to the Presbyterian College to be trained for the
ministry.

V

But her interest in Robert's future, as well as her
interest in Alec's shop, was suddenly dispersed by her
discovery that Mattie, without a word to her, had
engaged herself to marry Andrew Shillington. Andrew
came to her, proposing an immediate marriage with
Mattie, and was pooh-poohed.

"The child's over young to be married," she said.

"Child!" Andrew exclaimed. "There's not much
of the child about her. She's nineteen an' a bit
more!"

"I'm busy," said Mrs. Dunwoody, cutting him short.

"But——"

"I'll think about it mebbe in two or three years' time."

"Two or three years' time! Sure, we might all be dead an' buried then," he remonstrated.

"Well, if we are, there'll be no call for marryin'."

Andrew stood before her, angry and bewildered, while she did this job and that about the shop, and waited for her to relent, but when he saw that she was ignoring him, his Ulster obstinacy made him resolve to have done with discussion and to announce a decision. "Look here, Mrs. Dunwoody," he said very firmly, "I spoke to you about Mattie because I wanted to do the civil an' nice thing by you, but if you're not willin' to be reasonable an' do the civil an' nice by me, I'll not discuss the matter with you at all."

"I'm not askin' you to discuss it," she answered. "I'm tellin' you what my mind is."

"Well, your mind's not my mind, nor Mattie's either for that matter. Her and me's goin' to be married on it, Mrs. Dunwoody, an' the sooner you reconcile yourself to that fact, the better it'll be for the whole of us."

She turned round on him. "You can quit out of my shop, Mr. Shillington," she said, "just as quick as ever you like."

The formal address of "Mr. Shillington" startled and dismayed him. She had known him all his life and had never hitherto called him anything but "Andy." The formality broke him.

"But, Mrs. Dunwoody, mem——"

"That'll do," she interrupted. "I've said my say. In two or three years' time, mebbe, but now, no. An' mebbe not then."

It was at that moment that Mattie, agitatedly listening, came crying to her mother that she would be married then or never.

"I'm goin' to have him, ma," she said, "whatever you say."

Mrs. Dunwoody stared at her as if she could not credit her ears.

"Are you demented, girl?" she demanded.

But Mattie remained firm. She seized Andrew's hand in hers, as if to reassure herself, and then boldly faced her mother. Her voice quavered as she spoke, but the quavering did not denote a failing purpose.

"I'll marry him now," she solemnly said, "as sure as there's a God above me. An' I dare you to stop me."

"That's the spirit," Andrew murmured, but Mrs. Dunwoody immediately silenced him. "Hold your tongue, you!" she said to him. "This is a matter for me an' my daughter."

"Ah, but it's me she's marryin'," he said in a lapsing voice as he stood aside.

Mrs. Dunwoody leant her elbows on the counter and adjusted her spectacles. She steadily gazed at Mattie for a few moments without speaking. Then she said, "You're determined to marry him, girl?"

"Yes, ma," Mattie answered without flinching.

"Whatever I say or do?"

"Whatever you say or do, ma—though I'd rather not offend you. But I'll have him now, ma," she hurriedly added, as if she were afraid she might be thought to be weakening.

"But what's the hurry?" Mrs. Dunwoody asked, after a pause.

"No hurry, except that we want to be married." It was Andrew who said this.

Mrs. Dunwoody was silent for a little while.

"Well?" said Andrew.

"Can you keep a wife?" she asked.

"Aye, I can, an' save a bit too," he confidently replied.

She turned away, and for a few moments pretended to arrange china ornaments on a shelf. She must think of something. . . . But Mattie was insistent. "Well, ma? Are you goin' to consent?" she demanded.

"Don't hurry me, girl," Mrs. Dunwoody said, without looking round. She took one of the ornaments in her hand—a piece called a "Sevastopol" and supposed to represent the gates of the besieged town—and turned it over and examined it. Why was she being so hard with the girl? Andrew was a decent enough lad. Was it because they had made a decision without her authority? Why could she not be kind to them, the young pair, so fond of each other? Any one with half an eye in his head could see how they loved each other. Why was she being so hard on them? . . . She scattered her thoughts, and put the ornament back in its place.

"I'll give my consent," she said, "if you'll both come and live here after you're married."

Andrew sulked. "We want a house of our own," he said. "Don't we, Mattie?"

"Yes, Andy," Mattie replied.

"An' forby," he continued, "it would look as if I couldn't earn enough to pay for a house, but had to get you to keep me!"

"That's my last offer," said Mrs. Dunwoody.

But if she was obstinate, so were they, and in the

end they were married without her consent or blessing.
They had disregarded her wishes and had broken up
her family, and she could not forgive them. She was
not present at their wedding, nor would she permit
Margaret to go to it. Alec was ordered to attend to
his business in Cromac Street! . . . Very bare and
friendless was the wedding, for Andrew and Mattie felt
that they could not indulge in show when her mother
ignored the marriage. Mattie made her poor finery as
best she could, and on the morning of her marriage,
dressed herself, though her eyes were aching with
unshed tears, and when she was ready she descended
from the attic which she shared with Margaret and
entered the shop where her mother was standing behind
the counter. She winced when she saw her, and for a
moment or two it seemed that Mrs. Dunwoody would
relent. But neither of them spoke. They stood there,
gazing at each other, the young girl beautiful in her
wedding-dress, and waited for a word to be uttered.
But it was not uttered, and each of them hardened her
heart. Margaret stood at the foot of the stairs, crying,
and Mattie turned to comfort her. "It's all right,
Maggie," she said. "I'm—I'm——"

She did not trust herself to finish the sentence, but
turned again to her mother. Her lips trembled as she
said, "I'm goin', ma!"

"So I see," said Mrs. Dunwoody.

But Mattie did not move. "Ma," she said, with
infinite pleading in her voice.

Mrs. Dunwoody's hand trembled and she took hold
of the counter to steady herself. All this, because the
boy and girl wanted to marry each other and had not
been tactful enough to do just what she wanted them

to do. How beautiful Mattie looked! The poor wee girl going out to get married and no woman to go with her. . . .

Then Mrs. Dunwoody heard herself saying, "You'll be keeping Mr. Shillington," and felt herself turning away from her daughter.

Mattie went out of the shop, with her head up, though a tear or two did fall. She heard Margaret trying to follow her, and the quick order of her mother, "Come here, girl!" and the sudden silence as her sister stopped, but she heard it very distantly. She must not cry. She must not meet Andrew with tears in her eyes! . . . And so, smiling, she went to Mr. Cregan's church and was married. But not quite without her family, for when the marriage was over and the register had been signed, and Andrew and she, now husband and wife, came down the empty-sounding aisle, suddenly from a pew she heard her name called. "Mattie! Mattie!" She looked round and saw Robert. She left her husband and ran to her brother and hugged him. "Oh, thank you, Darkie dear," she said, and now her pride all down, she cried without pretence.

"You're a brave dacent wee fellow," said Andrew Shillington.

Robert looked up at them. "I mitched," he said. "I mitched from school."

"You shouldn't 'a' done that," Mattie murmured, smiling at him as she wiped her eyes.

"I'll get the quare oul' skelpin' for it when I get home," Robert said, "but sure I don't care. Somebody had to be here."

He went home when Andrew and Mattie had gone off to Pickie for their day's honeymoon. Mrs. Dunwoody stared at him with strange, dry eyes as he entered the shop.

"Why aren't you at your school?" she said.

"I didn't go to school," he answered. "I mitched. I went to see Mattie married."

He waited for her anger to break on him, but her voice was unexpectedly gentle when she spoke.

"Come here, wee son," she said, and when he approached her, she put her arm around his neck and drew him very close to her.

"I'm glad some one was there," she said.

"Why didn't you go yourself then?" he asked.

She turned away. "I'd 'a' give the world to be there," she said

VI

Her desire that she might have been present at Mattie's marriage did not reconcile her to Mattie's disobedience. She made her will the more inflexible because her heart urged her to yield to the young—"if I'm soft with her I'll mebbe have to be soft with Robert!"—and so there was no communication between her and her daughter for several months after the marriage. She knew that Robert saw Mattie, nor did she try to prevent him from seeing her, but she sternly forbade Margaret and Alec to visit or mention her. Alec obeyed her, but she had trouble with Margaret who, in the end, reconciled her to Mattie. One night, six months after the marriage, Margaret slipped out of the shop when her mother was too busily engaged with customers to see what she was doing. She ran all the way to the short, ill-lit street of kitchen-houses to which Andrew Shillington had taken his bride. It was a new street, mainly inhabited by young working-men and their young wives, and in spite of its mean look it had an air of adventure and hope and romance. Not yet had its essential ugliness worn down the spirits of the young couples who lived in it. That would come later, too soon. In a little while the mean-minded rich who housed their labourers in this dingy and hideous street would have robbed these young of their romance and their happy aspirations, but that time was not yet. The little red houses were as new as the love that lived in them and seemed like it to be lovely. Each house had a patch of mouldy earth in front of the kitchen-window, about six feet in length and three feet in breadth. An iron railing, resting on a shallow foundation of red bricks, separated the garden from the cobbled pavement. Andrew had sown seed that was mostly infertile in his "garden," and here and there a patch of grass struggled out of the sour soil. Nasturtiums, unquenchably gay, climbed up a length of string to the window, and a clump of faded chrysanthe-mums, smutted over with soot, leant against the spout which dropped the rain from the roof to the ground. Margaret, remembering the brightness of her mother's shop and the comfort of the rooms, shivered as she turned into the dark little street. Her heart unaccount-ably failed her as she reached Mattie's house, and she hesitated before the door. Then she compromised with her obedience, and climbed on to the brick foundation between the garden and the foot-path, and, holding on to the iron railing, peered through the kitchen-window and saw her sister lifting a heavy kettle on to the hob. "She's made it look quare an' nice," she murmured to herself, and indeed the kitchen had a

warm, bright, snug look, despite its bareness. Andrew
had not yet returned from his work, but presently
would do so, and Mattie was laying the table for their
evening meal. The kettle was nearly too heavy for
her to lift, and when she had shifted it from the hob
to the hot coals, she straightened herself with an air
of weariness and turned away from the fire. She was
crying. The young face was not now so pretty as it
had been, but was drawn and tired and white. She
stood irresolutely between the table and the fire, and
then suddenly and heavily sat down and abandoned
herself to her misery. Margaret trembled outside,
unable to bear the sight of her sister in tears, and she
dropped from the railing to the ground and stood in
a bewildered state before the door. She felt that her
mother ought to be comforting Mattie, but she longed
to rush into the kitchen herself and throw her arms
around her sister and weep with her. She moved
towards the door, but stopped before she had reached
it, and then, as suddenly as she had run out of the
shop, she ran back to it. It seemed to be full of
customers when she returned, and she caught a
reproachful look from Mrs. Dunwoody, but Margaret
paid no heed to the customers. She hurried behind the
counter and panted her news into her mother's ears.

"Mattie's goin' to have a child," she said, "an' she's
sittin' up there by her lone, cryin' her eyes out!"

A customer gaped at her as if she were mad, but
Margaret did not care what the customer thought.
She waited for her mother to speak. Mrs. Dunwoody
stared at her for a few moments, and then took off her
shop-apron and threw it aside.

"Get me my bonnet an' shawl," she said, and Mar-

garet flew upstairs to obey her. When she returned
the customers were gone. "You served them brave
an' quick, ma!" said Margaret, putting the shawl about
her mother's shoulders.

"Aye," Mrs. Dunwoody answered. "Shut the shop,
girl!"

"What about Alec and Darkie? . . ."

"Robert's away playin' himself. He can play a bit
longer, an' Alec's able to look after himself. Shut
the shop."

When the lamps were extinguished, and the shop-
door was closed, they hurried off together to Mattie's
house. They did not speak, except once when Mrs.
Dunwoody said, "How do *you* know she's goin' to have
a child?" and Margaret replied, "Och, I know rightly!"
The street seemed darker to Margaret than it was a
little earlier in the evening; the foggy, yellow light
from the gas-lamps lit only small patches of it. She
led her mother to Mattie's door and was about to enter,
but Mrs. Dunwoody caught hold of her arm and
restrained her. "Wait a bit," she said, and climbed on
to the railings and peered in at the window as Margaret
herself had done. Andrew was now at home, and he
was kneeling on the floor beside Mattie, with his arms
round her, trying to soothe her distress. But she could
hardly be comforted, and the anxiety on his face showed
that he was nearly as cheerless as Mattie. Mrs. Dunwoody looked at them, and then a cry forced itself
from her lips, and she dropped from the railings and
ran into the hall and flung open the door, leaving Margaret gaping after her. She rushed into the kitchen,
crying "Come here to me, daughter!" and took Mattie
in her arms and covered her face with kisses.

"They were both cryin' hard when I went in," said Margaret, when she told the story afterwards to Alec, "but God knows it was a different sort of a cryin' this time from the sort Mattie was at when I saw her the first time through the window."

THE THIRD CHAPTER

I

IT seemed then to Mrs. Dunwoody that life was smoothly set for her. The shop and its branch steadily flourished. She had her wish that Mattie's son should be born in her house, for Andrew Shillington had submitted to her plea that a labourer's cottage was not a proper place for a Dunwoody child with De Lacy blood in its veins to be born in. The birth of the boy elated her, and she promised to furnish a better house for the young parents than the one in which they had started married life. Andrew and she, while searching for a house, talked about the baby and his mother, and imperceptibly Andrew received her affection. She liked his decision and his uprightness and his obstinacy when he had satisfied himself that a thing must be done. She had to give reasons to him, and although she preferred to give commands, she was content. "He'll tame Mattie anyway," she said to herself. They found a new home for Mattie in a parlour-house in a street near the shop, so near that Mrs. Dunwoody could walk to it in a few moments. This was now her chief pleasure, and gradually she relaxed her control over the shop, entrusting it more and more to Margaret while she indulged herself in her love for her grandchild. As she sauntered to Mattie's house, she allowed her fancy to run away with her. Mattie's marriage had jolted

her, and for a little while she was afraid, but all was
well. Mattie had returned to her obedience, and was
now a purring, contented mother, with no wild desire
for flight or self-will. Andrew's mind was not unlike
Mrs. Dunwoody's; their desires were akin. She was
satisfied with Mattie's marriage, was even pleased with
it. Andrew would certainly be a master one of these
days. He was not one of the sort that remained a
serving-man. There was much nonsense being talked
around her by wild fellows, but she had lived a life
and had observed men and women, and she knew that
some were born to be masters and some were born to
be servants. They could talk their heads off, but they
could not talk that fact away. Andrew Shillington was
serving now, but only until he had learnt his trade as
a master, and when that time was over, he would take
his proper place. She was well pleased with Andrew.
Nor was her content only with Andrew and Mattie.
Sam Peden showed signs of liking Margaret, and her
secret hope had always been that Sam Peden would
marry either Margaret or Mattie. Sam Peden was no
fool; he had his father's ability and a bit more of his
own. There was no knowing where Sam would land,
once he started going. Not for the world would she
show signs or countenance to Sam or Margaret of what
she hoped and desired. The pair of them were well
able to look after themselves! . . . It was Robert that
bothered her mind. He remained her darling, despite
the rivalry of his nephew. Would he continue to please
her as he was presently doing? She was not sure of
him, and of him, more than of her other children, she
ardently desired to be sure. Each morning, she saw
him depart for Martin's College with pride which she

could not express, and vaguely, reluctantly she realised that he was reaching out to manhood. In a year or two he would leave Martin's and go to the Presbyterian College, and then, if she were spared and God were willing, her wish would be fulfilled; she would "sit under" her son and be greeted by his congregation as "the minister's mother." When her mind turned back on her life, it found few dark patches and many that were bright. The hard times must have seemed harder while she was enduring them than they really were. Odd, now, that misfortune should make so poor a show in the memory, while good times glowed! Here, anyhow, was a settled, sober and satisfying life. If it continued, she could, when her time came to leave it, do so with content, knowing that God had dealt fairly by her! . . .

She did not lose her faith in the fair dealing of God when the sudden blow of Andrew Shillington's death fell upon her. He had come very close to her love, but there was comfort even in his loss, for Mattie and her son came home again. All her children were under her roof now, and one child more; the little Andrew. She had serenity, and serenity had sometimes seemed likely to be denied to her for ever. Alec and Margaret, with help from the widowed Mattie, persuaded her to relax her labours, and, not unwillingly, she would sometimes sit at the shop-door taking the sun and the air, while the baby Andrew slept by her side. Her memory began to be busy with her youth, and she felt odd longings to visit people whom she had known when she was young. She remembered her roots, and suddenly she announced to her family that she was in the mind to go to Donaghreagh for a rest. It was years, she said, since she had been there, and a desire came over her to see it again. Robert had stayed in Donaghreagh fewer times than any of them, so she would take him with her. The rest could come down for the day on Sunday. They were mystified by her sudden decision, but it held no mystery for her. She felt her roots pulling at her heart; Donaghreagh was the soil in which she had grown. That was all.

II

The journey was like an exile's return to his native country. She recovered names and places that she had forgotten and took a queer delight in telling them over to Robert. When the train ran into Ballyards and she caught the first glimpse of Lough Cuan, recollection overflowed her mind and she brought Robert to her side at the window, while she recalled aloud what she remembered of the country through which they were travelling. "Lord Castlederry has his demesne round there," she said, pointing to the eastern side of the lough, "an' if you walk along the shore towards his place you'll see a big rock standin' on the edge of the water. They call it the Butter Lump in the books, but it was always called the Big Stone when I was a girl, though some people that was addicted to gamblin' used to call it the Giants' Jack! That's where I first saw your father, Robert. He was lyin' up against it, an' he passed a remark to me. I give him a very cool answer, for I was well brought up an' taught not to be too free with strangers. You see, I was only over there from Donaghreagh for the day. But he wasn't a bit put out by the short answer he got, an' he started to gag

me. I couldn't stand out against him, he had such
a comic tongue in his head. 'You're quare an' stiff,'
says he. 'Anybody'd think you were Lady Castlederry
herself, you're that grand on it!' I was never one
ready with my answer to people, but I was ready for
him. 'Ah,' says I, 'an' how do you know I'm not
Lady Castlederry?' He was as ready for me as I was
for him. 'I know rightly," he said. 'I wouldn't have
the nerve to address you if you were. She's a terrible
proud woman, that!' 'An' amn't I proud, too?' says I.
'Oh, proud enough,' he answered me, comin' away
from the Butter Lump that was rubbin' his coat smooth
an' shiny, an' standin' fornenst me. 'I suppose,' says
he, smilin' at me, 'if I was to walk as far as the town
with you, you'd ate the head off me?' "

Robert interrupted his mother. "Do you mean to
say he struck up to you, ma?"

"Aye, son," she shyly answered, "he struck up to me.
I didn't dare to think what your gran'ma would 'a' said
about it, but I never toul' her about it, so she suffered
no hurt."

"Your father was a great lad for coddin' an' gaggin',"
she continued. "You couldn't be in his company without wantin' to be coddin' an' gaggin' yourself. Have
you never noticed, son, the way you catch pleasure
from some people? It's as if they were smittle. Your
father was like that. The place was brighter for him.
I'm not a great woman for jokes an' talk, but even I
got chatty an' comic when your father was in the house.
I had my answer for him, too, when he asked me if
I'd ate the head off him if he dandhered along by the
side of me. I turned to him as sharp as you like, an'
I said, 'I'm very partic'lar what I eat!' I wish you

could 'a' heard the roar he let out of him when I said that. He was as pleased as if he'd said it himself an' indeed it wasn't bad, considerin' it was me that made it. He fell into step with me, an' we walked back the len'th of the road thegether, him sayin' every now an' awhile, 'You're the great girl for givin' back answers. I suppose you'd ate the head off me, says I. No, says she, I'm very partic'lar what I eat. Och, sang, but you're the great girl for givin' back answers!' That was the sort of conversation we had, son, him an' me, an' he left me feelin' that well pleased with me, that I was pleased with him, too. 'So long,' says he, when we separated, 'I'll mebbe see you again?' 'An' mebbe you'll not,' says I, 'for I'm seldom in Ballyards. Donaghreagh's where I live.' 'Is it?' says he. 'Whereabouts?' I just tossed my head at him, an' I said, 'It might be in the Manor House an' it might be in the Poor House.' I was just in the mood for coddin' him like that, son. 'Well, where do you live?' says he. 'You'd better come an' fin' out,' was all the answer he got out of me. 'By my sang,' says he, 'I will. I'll be there Saturday's a week, an' mebbe you'll keep an eye open for me.' 'Oh, I don't know so much about that,' says I. 'You'll have to do all the lookin' yourself. I'm not goin' to demean myself lookin' out for any fella.' He took it well. 'I'll be there Saturday's a week,' says he, an' he was. I was married on him six months later. He was a darin' fella was your father, an' my heart's joy."

She pointed to Knock Scraboh. "Do you see thon hill?" she said. "Him an' me walked up it the day we were married. It was all the honeymoon we had, but I enjoyed it better nor any high-up woman ever enjoyed her trips abroad. It's a long time now, Robert, since I lost your father, but I can see him as plain as I can see you, an' I never rued a minute I was with him. I wish he was here now, goin' back to Donaghreagh with me, the way he used to when he come back from a voyage an' I'd go to Belfast to meet him."

She became silent, and remained silent until the train drew up in Donaghreagh station, and during that silence Robert's mind revolved around the father whom he had never seen. He was a sea-faring man! . . . But he did not speak to his mother of what was in his thoughts. Rain was falling when they alighted from the train into a station which looked like part of a private house. The engine seemed to be standing in a back-room.

"This is a queer sort of a station!" Robert exclaimed, glancing round the bare buildings. "The County down must 'a' been very hard up when they stuck this up."

She thought he was slighting her birth-place. "It's a very nice wee station," she said sharply, "far better nor any of your slap-up, grand places. It makes you feel homely, anyway, an' no other station ever I was in makes you feel that way. We'll walk up now to our lodgin's an settle ourselves, an' then mebbe we'll take a bit of a walk roun' the town——"

"Town!" Robert laughed. "I like the town. Sure, it's only a cod of a place. You could put it in a corner of Belfast an' never know it was there."

"You've a strange notion of a joke, Robert. It doesn't become you to talk that way of the place where your people come from. An' let me tell you this place was notorious long before ever Belfast was known or heard of. You're greatly set up on your Belfast, but the world knows well that it's a mushroom sort of a town by the side of Donaghreagh. Just consider that, my son."

He teased her. "You're lossin' your temper," he said.

"No, I'm not——!"

"Och, yes, you are, ma. Your hand's tremblin' with the rage you're in."

"I'm not, I tell you, but I take pride in my place an' I like them that belong to me to take pride in it, too. This is a great wee town, though mebbe you can't recognise its greatness. Look there," she said, as they paused at the station-door while she pointed to the harbour and the Three Islands lying a mile out in Knock Fergus Bay. "Isn't that a lovely sight?"

"Och, I don't know——!"

"You know rightly, but you'll not admit it. You're in one of your provokin' moods an' you'll go against everybody an' everything."

He saw that she was hurt and angry, and he sobered himself. "I'm not tryin' to provoke you at all, ma," he said. "I just don't think much of it. I never did think much of it. I'd rather have Pickie any day."

"Pickie!" she said in a contemptuous tone.

"Well, there's a bit of life there any way. They're all dead in this place, an' there's nobody to bury them."

Anxiety filled her. "Do you really not like it, Robert?" she said.

"It's all right in its way, but anybody'd think it was heaven, from your talk. I'm not taken with it, but of course I'm only at the station yet, an' the rain's pourin' down. I dare say when I get used to it, I'll think more of it. It's not too bad."

She made no answer to this, but started off towards the lodgings she had rented. She had hoped that Robert would feel affection for Donaghreagh as deep as her own, but his mockery of it, although she felt that most of it was meant to tease her, made her realise that he looked at it more critically than she did. She blamed herself for not having brought him more frequently to the village in his childhood. She remembered now with regret that when Robert had proposed to her once that she should take them to "the shore" for a month, she had scornfully refused to follow the example of her neighbours who could not content themselves in their own homes. If Robert had scrambled about the rocks of Donaghreagh in his childhood, he would now have affectionate recollections of it and would not be tormenting her with his belittlement. But he had no young memories to lean on.

Their lodging was on the Shore Road, midway in the bend of the bay, and standing at the door they could see the lighthouse at the end of the pier, and immediately in front of them, the largest of the Three Islands. The drift of rain hid the coast of Scotland from them, but they saw ships on the Irish Sea, and, far out on the horizon, the smoke of an Atlantic liner.

"That's fine enough for you, isn't it?" she said, when they had bestowed their trunks in the bedrooms and were gazing out of the window. "Where in the earthly world could you get better views nor here? Isn't it just like the kingdoms of the world spread out fornenst your eyes? The Moat's a wee pace from the door. Will you come an' see it?"

"Och, I've seen it once, ma. An' the street's wet."

"The rain's stopped. Come just to oblige me an'

see it again. The tea's not ready yet, an' we'll have
time an' plenty to walk to the Moat an' back."

They walked along the road to the narrow lane
which led to a large, steep dun with a square, castel-
lated building on its summit, which was called "The
Moat." She did not speak as they climbed the narrow,
slippery path, but waited for some words of admiration
from him. He stood erect, when they were on top of
the dun, and gazed at the ramshackle building on it.

"They ought to pull this place down," he said.

She could not bear it. She sat down on a wooden
seat, and he was shocked at the anger he saw in her
eyes.

"What ails you?" he asked.

"Ails me! You an' your talk!——"

"But——"

"Wheesht, wheesht with you, an' think shame of
yourself. It's all that's left of the oul' ancient days
and you want to pull it down. For shame, Robert
Dunwoody, for shame."

He thrust out his under lip. "Well, sure, it's ugly,"
he began, but she stopped him.

"It's oul'," she said. "No one knows how oul'
it is."

"What differs does that make? It's oul' an' ugly,
an' I see no sense in keepin' an ugly thing just acause
it's oul'."

"Generations of people have sat here the way we're
sittin', an' looked over the sea as we're lookin' now.
Is that nothin' to you, Robert, nothin' at all? Your
people climbed this bit of a hill many's a time! . . .
Look, look at the way people's cut their names all over
the place. You'll find our name plenty of places here.

Why, I came here as a wee slip of a girl an' rowled down the hill into the *shough,* an' I thought it was the most wonderful place on God's earth. An' you want to pull it down."

"Sure, it's tumblin' to pieces," he said in a resentful tone, for her distress made him uneasy. "An' what's the good of it anyway?"

"The good of it!" she exclaimed. "This good! To mind people of them that went before them, an' to make them feel a pride in their family an' their generation. That's the good of it, an' he's a poor sort of a fellow that has to be told it."

"Well, I don't see much sense in it," he retorted.

They descended from the Moat and returned to their lodgings. "It's all lovely," she said, "every inch of it."

The tide was out, and yellow weed lay in lank heaps about the strand.

"The foreshore looks terrible dirty," said Robert.

She started away from him. "I'm sorry I brought you," she said.

III

Her spirits recovered when she found that although he disliked the village or, as she preferred to call it, the town, he delighted in the country round it, and she encouraged him to take the long, lonely walks he liked about the Peninsula. He would follow the roads past fine farms until at last he landed on the shores of Lough Cuan where he would lie down and sun himself in full view of Knock Scraboh or see the Mourne Mountains darkly rising through clouds to the sky. To come on Lough Cuan when the tide was out was his chief pleasure. Suddenly the Lough would empty itself into the Irish Sea, leaving a wide stretch of green and red mud, fringed by black rock and masses of yellow sea-weed. Birds picked their way through the weed and the rock-pools, bewildering him with their variety and teasing him because he could not name them. He climbed to the top of the Butter Lump, where his mother had first met his father, and sat there in an ecstacy because there was so much loveliness in the world. Sometimes, when the air was wet with rain, and the trees and grass became acutely green, he felt that he could not bear to go away, that he must remain in this place until he died. A love of earth, of familiar soil, began to grow in his heart, and he would stretch himself on the Butter Lump and gaze at Knock Scraboh and the vari-coloured bed of Lough Cuan and the high, piercing black peaks of Mourne as if they were living creatures that he might fondle. He felt an anger, which he could not explain, when he saw that some religious fanatic had painted "Prepare to meet Thy God," in large white letters on one side of the Butter Lump, and "Eternity" on the other. Why could they not leave the Butter Lump alone? Reluctantly, in the evening, he would return to Donaghreagh, suddenly saddened at the sight of so much beauty disappearing in the darkness. Mrs. Dunwoody was persuaded to ride on a long car with him down the length of the Peninsula, through Ballywater and Cloey to Ballyquin-lan Point and Ferryport and up the Lough Cuan side through Greycubbin and Kirk Abbey and Ballyards to Donaghreagh again. Wherever they went, they found great masses of yellow sea-weed, trailing across the rocks.

"Quare stuff," said Robert, gazing at it in a puzzled manner. "I can't bear it, an' yet I love to look at it. It's sad-lookin'."

"You're not afeard of sorrow, son?" Mrs. Dunwoody murmured.

"Afeard of sorrow!" he replied. "I don't understand you, ma!"

She paused a moment. "No, son, of course not. But don't be afeard of it when it does come." Her tone changed, becoming brighter. "You like the country now, don't you?" she said, and she meant by "the country" this one part of the earth that was hers.

"I like it well enough," he answered.

"Do you not love it?"

He considered. "Aye, I do," he said.

"Aren't you glad your family come from a place as nice as this—all this nice land an' the fine-lookin' farms an' the dacent people? Look roun' you, son. It's a lovely wee place, isn't it?"

"It is," he said.

"Where in the earthly world would you see any place as nice as this? All them wee hills, now, would they be any better anywhere else? You wouldn't want to go away from this, son, would you? You'd be content to stay here all your life, with your friends an' your relations?"

"I don't know so much about that, ma."

She did not continue the conversation in those terms, but contented herself with repeating his praises of the Peninsula. Very slyly, as she thought, she belittled foreign countries by exalting her own. In the evening, when they had eaten their tea, she took him up the road to Killisland, and when they had reached the Presby-

terian church, she stopped him outside the railings and
bade him look inside.

"I'd give the world," she said, "to see you in the
pulpit of that place. The Reverend Robert Dunwoody!"

He faced her then. "I don't want to be a minister,"
he said.

"But, son, I intend you for one——"

"I tell you, ma, I'd hate it. I'm not the minister
sort!——"

Her voice hardened as she interrupted him. "An'
what sort are you? What *do* you propose to do with
yourself?"

"I said before," he answered, "I want to go to sea
like my father. I'm just longin' to be on a boat——"

"Come home," she said bitterly.

She hurried away from the church, back to their
lodgings, nor did she seem to know that he was not
following her. For a few moments, he stood in front
of the church-railings, gazing after her as she walked
down the sloping street, half eager to run after her and
make her happy by agreeing to her wish, half resentful
against her because she tried to subdue him to her ambition. While he deliberated, she turned a corner and
was out of sight. He rebuked himself for his obstinacy.
Suddenly she had seemed an old, old woman to him as
she picked her way down the rough, descending foot-
path. There was a frail look about her that made him
feel tender to her. His mind filled with her story, how
she had striven with hardship that her children might
be made safe from it. Alec, sometimes in the attic,
would repeat it to him and say, "She has the heart of
a hundred men, that woman!" And so, indeed, she

had. His love for her swiftly surged up like the inrushing tide of Lough Cuan, as he stood there remembering her slight, determined figure, bending now with her age and her disappointments, and he wanted to cry. Very deeply he loved his mother, yet no one roused in him so much opposition as she did. Why could he not obey her, or at least pretend that he would some day fulfil her ambition, when he loved her more than he was able to say? He turned towards the church, and leant against the railings, so that his tears might not be observed by passers-by, and presently he heard himself talking as if she were standing by his side. "You know, I love you," he was saying, "but you keep on makin' me resist you as if I didn't love you at all. Anybody, to hear me refusin' you when you want me to be a minister, 'ud near think I hated you, but you *know* I love you, an' what do you keep on makin' me look as if I didn't for?" Then he talked to himself, as if he realised that she had left him. "Why don't you follow her home an' tell her you'll do any dam' thing she wants, even if you hate doin' it, just because you can't bear her to be unhappy——"

He wiped his eyes, and turned away from the church, and stood on the kerb for a few moments, undetermined what to do. Then he walked along the road to Killisland, away from Donaghreagh.

IV

An old church, very small, was perched on the edge of the sea, and Robert climbed over the wall and walked through the graveyard in which mouldering headstones recorded the names of the long-ago dead.

While he stood before one of the graves, endeavouring to decipher the worn names on the stone, he heard voices, and presently round the corner of the tiny church, coming from the sea, Brenda Cairnduff and a girl, strange to Robert, appeared. Brenda came quickly to him. "Is that you, Darkie?" she said, holding out her hand. "I didn't expect to see you here."

She introduced him to her companion, a cousin, and he explained his appearance in Killisland.

"I'm just down for the day," she said. "I'm going back to Belfast to-night. I'm really on my way to the station now. My cousin here is leaving me part of the way to Donaghreagh, but if you're going back now, you could save her the trouble."

"Well, I wasn't goin' just yet——"

"Of course," she interrupted, "I don't want to take you out of your way, but I just thought I'd like to step in and say good-evening to your mother. But if you don't want to keep me company——"

She did not finish the sentence, contenting herself with a sly smile. Her cousin settled the matter in a quick, decisive way. "Well, as you won't want me any more," she said, "I think I'll just turn back now. I've a lot to do before bedtime. Good-night, Brenda!" She kissed Brenda and shook hands with Robert. "Any time you're passin' this way," she said to him, "call in, an' we'll be glad to give you a drop of tea."

"You're very kind——"

"Good-night, then!" and she turned and went quickly back to the village.

Brenda regarded her cousin in silence until she was out of hearing. Then she said to Robert, "Mamie's a nice girl, but she's very country. She has an awful broad way of talking, and she's terribly off-hand in her manners."

"Sure, there's no harm in that, Brenda."

"You're not so particular as I am, Darkie, I know. You might be a lot more particular with advantage. But then things are very different for a man. He can afford not to be so particular as a woman. A woman has to be more particular——"

He interrupted her. "Here's a cart comin'," he said. "You can get a lift back to Donaghreagh."

"Darkie," she said, indignantly, as they looked towards the approaching farm-cart, "you know I'd never go in a thing like that. What would anybody think if they saw me in a cart? It wouldn't be the thing at all. No, we'll walk and we'd better start at once. If anything comes along—nice, I mean—we'll mebbe get a lift on it, but I'm quite content to walk."

"Have it your own way," he replied, as they left the churchyard and turned towards Donaghreagh. "Though what's wrong with the cart I can't see."

"No, of course not." She smiled at him indulgently. "You were always a wee bit rough and ready, Darkie. You really ought to start thinking about things in a more refined way. You'll soon be a grown man." He grunted, but did not speak. She heaved a sigh of satisfaction. "It's awfully nice to see you again, Darkie," she said. "I haven't had a walk with you for a long while."

"I dare say you had better company. Alec's always ready to take you anywhere you want to go."

She shrugged her shoulders. "Alec!" she said, with a little contempt in her tone which he resented.

"What's the matter with Alec?" he demanded.

"He's a good fella—looks after himself—an' any girl ought to be glad of the chance of goin' with him?"

"Of course, I'm not making little of Alec—not in the very least—but I'm not very much in the notion of him."

"You could do worse—a lot worse. Come on, step it out or you'll miss your train."

She made a face in her impatience and irritation. "Really, Darkie," she said, "you're a most provoking person. I haven't seen you for I don't know how long and already you want to get rid of me. I've plenty of time for my train, and even if I miss it, what matter. I could stay the night in Donaghreagh. My mother will think I'm staying with Mamie. Mebbe, Mrs. Dunwoody could get me a room in your lodgings——"

"There isn't a room in the house!"

She blushed with vexation. "Anybody'd near think you didn't want me," she said.

"Now, don't be foolish, Brenda," he replied. "It doesn't matter one way or the other to me."

"Sometimes, I think you don't like me," she murmured.

"Och, I like you well enough. What's the matter with you?"

She did not answer, and they walked along in silence. The evening was closing in, and the boats which drifted on the sea began to put out their lamps. The sea was silent. Quietness came over the fields, as the birds and cattle settled down for the night. Brenda lifted her head and gazed about her, as if she were looking for some one, and then she slipped her arm in his. "I wish you would like me more," she said.

"What for?"

"You know rightly. You're just saying that to torment me. Wait a minute. Sit here a wee while!" She sat down on the low stone wall, as she spoke.

"You'll miss your train," he answered.

"Sit down beside me when I ask you. I'm tired."

He sat beside her. "You should 'a' took the lift when you could 'a' got it," he said.

"Darkie!"

"Yes."

"You're a queer fellow!"

"What's queer about me?" he demanded.

"Well, the way you go on. Amn't I nice?"

He regarded her with astonishment. "You're very nice," he replied.

"Well, why don't you? . . . Och, Darkie, are you provoking me or are you just thick?"

He got up and stood beside her. "I think you must be a bit upset or something. Come on!" But she did not rise.

"I want to tell you something," she said.

"Go on, then."

"But come nearer. I don't want the whole world to hear me."

"Sure, there's not a person within a couple of miles of you——"

She seized hold of his coat and drew him to her. "Bend down," she said, and when he had done so, she kissed him.

"There," she said. "That's what I've been wanting to do all the time, and I ought not to have had to do it. You should have kissed me. I love you, Darkie."

He compelled her to get up from the wall, and without speaking they continued on their way. She put her arm in his, and he did not resist her. Silently they came to Donaghreagh.

"You've just time to get your train," he said. "You'd better not come to see my ma."

"Very well," she answered.

He took her to the station and put her in the train. "Good-night, Brenda," he said.

"Do you not love me?" she asked.

"I don't love anybody," he replied, "except my ma."

"I don't mean that sort of love. Do you not love me the way a fellow loves his girl?"

"No, Brenda, I don't."

She sat back in her seat.

"Good-night," he said.

But she did not reply.

V

Mrs. Dunwoody and Robert returned to Belfast at the end of their holiday in some anger with each other. Their discussions, however they might start, ended with his obstinate assertion that he was determined to be a sailor.

"It's no use talking," she said, "I've planned your career!"

"Amn't I to have any say in it, then?"

"At your age. What do you know what you want? . . ."

The life in the shop was resumed where it had been left off. Alec came and went about the two shops, helped by Margaret, who was now allowed to "go up the road" with Sam Peden, but was forbidden to consider herself seriously engaged to him for a year or two. Robert returned to Martin's College. Soon he would be leaving it, his mother said, to go to the Presbyterian College. There was nonsense in his mind about a sea-faring life, but that was only a lad's nonsense. Presently, as his education improved and his judgment sobered, he would put such follies away and would be guided by her. The Dunwoody family would live in unity in the one place, admired and respected! . . . With this dream in her mind, she told Alec to take Robert to the exhibition which was opened in Belfast soon after her return from the expedition to Donagh-reagh. They were to pay particular attention to the useful exhibits, and Alec obeyed her introduction with an exactitude which bored his brother. Robert wanted to see the lady whose head was cut off and exposed on a plate and then restored to her body, but Alec insisted that he should look at machinery for crushing cake for cattle, and urged him to marvel at the extent and variety of the exports and imports of Ireland. "Sure, it's only a fraud!" he said, when Robert repeated his desire to see the decapitated lady. "Fancy the idea of paying sixpence to be humbugged, and you able to see all these great machines for nothing!" Robert hated machinery. He had never had the boy's love of it, and he could not be persuaded to go down to the engine-room of the paddle-steamer which ran from Belfast to Pickie because the smell of the hot oil and the noise of the plunging propellers were insufferable to him. He loved the deck and the sound of the scud and the smell of the sea, and he would stand as long as he could in the bows of the *Slieve Bearnagh* trying to catch white drops of foam as they flew past him on the wind, or watching the water being cut into great curves of green crystal as the boat drove through it. He could not excite himself about boilers and screws and binders and steam-ploughs, and Alec's suggestion that it would be very useful for him, when he was a minister, to be able to discourse with merchants in an intelligent, as well as a Christian, manner left him unimpressed. "The trouble with half the ministers," Alec said to Robert's unheeding ears, "is that they have no gumption about ordinary affairs. They blether away as if we were all livin' like Jews in Palestine and doin' our ploughin' with the help of cattle. There's not a one of them seems ever to have seen or heard of a steam-plough. Now, you pay attention to that, Robert, and you'll get the advantage of it. People in a big way of business'll heed you then, for they'll know you have a bit of wit and knowledge in your head. Do you see this thing here? One girl, standing at it, can do more work with it in a day nor a hundred men could do in a week with the oul' hand-looms——"

"I don't care a damn whether she can or not," said Robert.

This was the first time that he had ever said a bad word, and the sound of it, as it left his lips, startled him. It came out so easily, too, that he might have been in the habit of swearing. He glanced at his brother, and saw that Alec was shocked.

"That's no language for a man that's dedicated to the ministry," Alec said.

Robert became stubborn. "Isn't it?" he said. "Well, it's the sort of language they'll get from me if they make a minister of me. A while ago you were grumblin' because half the ministers had no gumption, and now you're grumblin' at me because I have. There's no contentin' you!"

"Cursin' and swearin' isn't gumption——"

"I dare say not, but all the people that has any gumption curses and swears. And damn's not much of a curse anyway. I've heard people, respected people, too, say a lot worse."

"There's no need for you to imitatin' the bad side of them. I'm not ignorant of the fact that people says things they'd do better not to say, but that's no reason why I should say them, an' it's no reason why you should. It would be a nice thing for a minister to go about the place damnin' and blastin' and then get up in the pulpit of a Sunday mornin' an' tell the people to have clean tongues!"

"Och, Alec, what harm's in a wee damn?"

"It's the beginnin' of a lot that's worse. Many's a man starts off with no more nor a damn an' ends up with D.T.'s an' the gallows. I tell you, boy, it's the start that matters. The rest is easy and natural. Now, take an interest in these machines and try to keep your mind off things that'll divert your thoughts."

Robert regarded his brother with curiosity. "Alec," he said, "did you never do nothin' wrong in your life?"

"I dare say I have. Many's a thing. But I do my best, and the best can do no more. Not that that'll bring you much reward. It's never the good and industrious man that's the favorite."

"What makes you think that?" Robert said.

"I've cause to think it," Alec answered mysteriously, and would not be any more explicit when Robert pressed him to explain himself.

The visit ended abruptly. Alec would not stay until

the hour of closing because he wished to go home and go to bed. "I have to get up in the mornin'," he said, "and attend to my work. I can't spend half the night here, galumphin' about!"

"I can't think what you come for if you want to run away the minute you arrive," Robert protested.

"I come because my ma told me to bring you. That's why I come. If you have any more remarks to make, make them when I'm not here."

VI

Margaret went with him on his next visit to the exhibition, which had now been open long enough for the novelty to have worn away. The authorities, hoping to revive interest in it, had engaged sensational "turns" which could be witnessed by all the visitors, not in the side-shows at an extra charge, but in the central hall as part of the cost of admission. On the night when Margaret and Robert went to the exhibition, the star performer was Blondin, the Frenchman who had crossed the Falls of Niagara on a tight-rope. Terrible tales were told of the risks which the Frenchman took. Other tight-rope walkers gave their performances with wide nets stretched beneath the rope to catch them if they should fall, but Blondin, although he was an old, gray-haired man, disdained to use a net. If he were to fall! . . . Margaret hardly dared to let her mind dwell on the horrid thought, and for a while refused to believe that Blondin, marvellous man though he was, would walk along a swaying rope high up in the air unless he had some protection from the floor beneath him, so Robert took her to the central hall

immediately they had paid for admission, to convince
her that there was no net. Up in the roof, at a dizzy
height, they could see a rope stretched between two
long poles, each of which was surmounted by a tiny
platform. The distance from the rope to the ground
seemed immense, and indeed it was considerable, and
while they contemplated it, they felt that nothing else
in the exhibition mattered but Blondin's performance.
Robert led Margaret to the platform at the end of the
hall where there were tiers of seats.

"It'll not begin for a long while yet," Margaret said,
but Robert did not reply. He sat down and motioned
to her to sit beside him.

"Don't you want to see the rest of the show?" she
asked.

"Not now," he replied. "We can see it after."

"But supposin' he falls down and kills himself—
we'll be in no mood then for walkin' round lookin' at
things," said Margaret.

"You can go if you like," he answered, "but
I'll wait here till he comes. I'll keep a seat for
you."

She went off, but did not stay away long, for she
found the exhibition tedious without the company of
some one to whom she could make remarks on it, and
so they sat together until the advertised hour when
Blondin was to ascend to the rope. The central hall
gradually filled, except in the middle, under the rope,
where a clear space was kept, "so that there should be
nothin' to stop him from hittin' the ground if he falls,"
as Margaret said. She glanced up into the roof where
the rope and the little platform could vaguely be seen
in the dusk, and shuddered at the thought of the calam-

ity which might occur. She felt herself turning dizzy with apprehension, and once she shivered violently. "Are you cold?" said Robert. She was ashamed to acknowledge that she was trembling with fear and she stoutly said "No" and held on to the seat to prevent herself from shuddering again.

"You're terrible calm," she said, just before the time when Blondin was to appear.

"Calm about what?" he asked.

"Him fallin' off that rope and smashin' himself to bits!"

"Och, that's girl's talk!" he scornfully exclaimed.

The lights were increased, and it seemed to Margaret, sitting on the platform and gazing down on the throng in the hall, that the place was full of animated footballs with staring eyes! She could see crowds of round, nodding heads which she wanted to kick! . . . Blondin came down the steps at the side of the platform from the room in which he dressesd for his performance. He passed close to Margaret and Robert, and they held their breath as he did so. He was now an old man with whitening hair and a full, fresh-coloured face. He walked heavily, but his strong eyes had a sleepy sort of strength in them such as is seen in the eyes of a wild animal. He wore a dark pink or pale red suit of "skinfits" or tights, from which a golden fringe dangled, and Robert thought he looked well in them, but Margaret said it was ridiculous for a man of his age to get himself up in that ludicrous fashion.

"How would you have him dressed—in a Sunday coat and trousers? Is that the way you'd have him walk the tight-rope?" Robert demanded.

"I don't want him to do it at all. Poor old soul,

it's fearful him having to earn his livin' that way at his age!——"

Bursts of applause greeted the old Frenchman as he came down to the platform, and he stood for a moment or two bowing to the audience, once to the right, twice to the centre, and once to the left. He bowed as if he were bored by the ceremony. One imagined him saying to himself, "I've come here to risk what's left of my life for your amusement and to provide myself with money. Let me get on with the job. Don't waste my time with your silly applause!"

He walked to the nearer of the two upright poles, and after a brief delay, was hauled to the roof in some kind of rope-cradle. They could see him standing on the platform in the roof, wiping his hands on a handkerchief and rubbing his shoes in powdered resin. The crowd became very silent, a great mass of upturned white faces. Then Blondin, taking the balancing-pole in his hands, stepped lightly on to the rope and strode across and back. The strain was over. Margaret no longer felt any desire to cry. The old Frenchman knew his job and was doing it superbly. Backwards and forwards he went across the rope in a glide that was very graceful. The swift, perfectly-poised figure, dexterously moving along the rope, seemed to be a different being from the old, gray-haired man who had walked so heavily across the platform, and Margaret could not easily reconcile the lithe rope-walker with the bulky old man who had brushed past her a few moments earlier. But Robert was entranced by him, and had no mind for speculations on his age or agility. He saw only the romantic figure, assuredly stepping on air. . . .

They watched him at his various tricks. He lay down full length on the rope. He crossed it, with his legs enveloped in a sack. He ran from one side to the other. He walked without the balancing-pole, keeping himself poised by his outstretched arms. He pushed a wheelbarrow in front of him. He pretended to fall. . . . Margaret sobbed at that moment, and Robert's heart leaped into his mouth, but he recovered himself quickly. "That's only a cod," he said to her. "He does that on purpose to scare you. Sure, that man would never fall!"

An official came to the front of the platform where Margaret and Robert were sitting and informed the audience that Blondin would now carry a man on his shoulders across the rope. Would any person present volunteer for this great honour? Silence was followed by nervous laughter and a pretence of offers from young men who were held back, without much difficulty, from the platform by their alarmed girls. A notoriously timid man was vainly urged by his friends to let Blondin carry him, and the look of dismay on his face denoted that he was afraid lest he might be taken against his will. Blondin, like a big, benignant bird, was resting with his balancing-pole lying before him on the arms of the tiny platform. The official still harangued the crowd. Was there not one man among them who would like to be able to tell his children and his children's children of the deed of daring he had done when he allowed Blondin, the greatest tight-rope walker in the world, to carry him across the rope? "With no net to catch you either!" Women drew in their breath when he said that. The words had a chastening effect on the audience, and the hilarious ceased to make any pretence to a daring they did not feel. The notoriously timid man was allowed to have reason on his side.

"Won't any one volunteer?" said the official in the accents of finality.

There was a short silence, and then Robert stood up. "Yes," he said. "I will."

VIII

The sensation was terrific. The official was the most astounded man in the hall, and he turned to Robert with a look on his face which indicated that he was about to dissuade him from his offer. "Do you mean it?" he said.

"I do indeed," Robert replied.

Margaret plucked at his arm. "For dear sake, Darkie," she began, but he pulled his arm away from her, and she turned to a woman beside her for support. "Persuade him," she said.

"Son, dear," said the woman, "are you away in the head or what? Sit down and content yourself. If the oul' fella up on the rope likes to chance his neck, let him. Sure, he's paid to do it. But you'll get nothin', except mebbe your skull cracked!"

"Och, it's all right," said Robert.

"Och, no, it's not——"

The official interposed between them. "You understand," he said, "that there's a great risk. Blondin's all right, but are you?"

"If he's all right," said Robert, "I am."

"It's easy to talk that way," the woman interrupted, "and you standin' on the ground, but how'll you talk when you're sittin' on his back and nothin' between you an' the floor but air!"

"I don't know what to do," began the bewildered official.

"Och, you know rightly what to do," said Margaret suddenly in possession of herself. "Forbid him to go up."

Robert rounded on her. "The man challenged anybody to let himself be carried over the rope, an' I made a fair offer——"

"Wasn't he only coddin'! Sure, they always say things like that, an' them knowin' well nobody'll heed them."

"As a matter of fact," the official explained, "that's true. We have a proper person who volunteers——"

"Then the whole thing's a fraud!" Robert indignantly demanded.

"Not at all. A man will be carried by Blondin, but if we were to let anybody go up—well, supposin' you lose your nerve half way across——"

"I won't," said Robert.

"You might. You'd be killed and so would Blondin!"

"I'll take my chance of that!"

Margaret plucked his arm again. "Darkie," she pleaded.

"Och, quit, Margaret," he said. "It's you that's put them all up to not lettin' me." He turned to the official. "I repeat my offer," he said. "I'm ready to go up, an' if you don't let me, you're a fraud."

There was some applause as he said this, but the majority of the audience were against him. One man tried to reassure his frightened wife by declaring that the whole thing was a put-up job. Robert overheard him, and indignantly answered him. "It's no put-up job," he exclaimed. "I've never clapped eyes on Blondin in my life before——"

"Well, the more damned fool you, then," said the man.

"Come on away, John!" said his wife, "for fear anything happens!"

But he would not listen to her. "I will not," he said. "I've paid my money, an' I'll see whatever there is to see!"

The official made his decision. He thought that that vast assemblage of enlightened people would support him in refusing to allow this young gentleman to endanger two lives! . . . The applause with which his statement was greeted convinced him that he had not judged the temper of the audience incorrectly. He would like to say that no one appreciated the courage and spirit of the young gentleman more than he did. A chorus of "Hear, hears!" and a single, "He's a bloody wee fool, an' ought to be well skelped!" interrupted this testimony to Robert. But, he continued, he could not be a party to endangering two lives, and therefore, he reluctantly refused to allow the young gentleman to carry out his intention. Nevertheless, Blondin would carry a man across the rope, and he was happy to say that there was some one present. . . .

Then a man employed by Blondin came forward, smiling and smirking, and proceeded to get ready for the adventure. He removed his boots, and was hauled to the platform by the rope which had previously hauled Blondin there. There had been a deep silence when Blondin first strode on to the rope, but now the silence was intense, despite the fact that every one knew that the man to be carried across was a paid employee of Blondin and accustomed to this performance. There was a pause, while Blondin and the man talked together. "He's tellin' him about you," said Margaret to her brother. Then, in silence, Blondin moved along the rope, with the man on his back and the balancing-pole in his hand. He moved slowly, feeling his way with great care, until he got to the middle of the rope, where he slowly knelt down and then slowly rose up again. He moved back a little then, and then went forward, and then . . . he slipped. Margaret's hands automatically rose to her face, and a long, indrawn "Oh!" broke from the audience, as if every man and woman in the crowd had become one person uttering a single cry. But Blondin recovered himself, and almost gaily ran across the rest of the rope where he dropped the man on the platform and left him. He turned then and strode back along the rope, and in a moment or two was down on the ground, while the great crowd cheered him. He climbed on to the platform where Robert and Margaret were sitting, and again he was the old, heavy man, with sweat pouring down his face. Excited men and women shook his hand, but he was indifferent to their applause. Robert stood up as he approached, and could almost smell the damp heat of his body.

"That's the wee fella that wanted you to carry him," said the woman who had supported Margaret.

Blondin stopped and looked at Robert. He held out his hand to him, and murmured words in French, and Robert, not knowing what to do, said, "Thank you, sir!" Then Blondin turned away and passed up the stairs to his dressing-room, nor did he turn his head for a moment to acknowledge the cheers that followed him. . . . There was some comic byplay with the man who had been left on the platform—a pretence that he could not get down, but Robert did not wait for the end of it.

"Come on," he said to Margaret "Let's go home now!"

Margaret followed him, and when they were out of the exhibition, she took hold of his arm. "My heart was in my mouth," she said, "that time he slipped. Weren't you afeard then, Darkie?"

"No," he said. "He did that on purpose. A man like that doesn't slip."

"Would you not have been afeard when you got up there? You might have turned giddy or something!"

He shook his head. "What would there be to be afeard of? Yon man's as sure-footed on a rope as you are on the ground."

"You've a terrible nerve, Darkie!"

"Och, no!"

They crossed the two bridges, stopping for a while on the second of them to look towards the harbour where they could see the lights of the cross-channel steamers. The wind blowing down from the lough came coolly across their cheeks.

"I'd love to be on one of them boats," said Robert.

"My ma'll never let you," Margaret replied

"I'll mebbe not ask her," he retorted.

They walked on towards the shop, and when they were nearly at the door, Robert turned to Margaret and said, "Don't say anything to her about me wantin' Blondin to carry me!"

"All right, Darkie," she answered, wondering why he made the request.

"It 'ud mebbe upset her," he added, as if he understood her thoughts. But the truth was that he was suddenly afraid of his mother.

IX

The news of Robert's exploit at the exhibition had already reached his mother. There were some among the audience who knew him, and they had hurried away to spread the news. "Do you know what Darkie Dunwoody done?" . . . It had come to her variously. One story was that Robert had been carried across the rope by Blondin and had narrowly missed falling! . . . When Margaret and Robert climbed the stairs to the return-room which was now the kitchen, they realised immediately they saw their mother that she knew what had happened. Her face was extraordinarily stern, and her eyes seemed suddenly to blaze when she saw her son.

"You born idiot!" she shouted at him, and the sound of her voice startled him, for she rarely shouted. "What sort of a way was that to behave? Makin' a show of yourself——"

He did not speak, but stood dumbly before her.

"An' you, Margaret," she continued, turning to her daughter, "what were you thinkin' to let him do it!"

"It wasn't her fault," Robert said. "She tried to stop me."

"Tried to stop you! You, at your age, actin' the child. Are you a want-wit or what?"

She paused, as if she expected him to reply, but he did not do so. He moved in a restive manner, and his breath began to come and go quickly.

"Stand still," she said, "an' answer me. You're a grown-up lad, near seventeen you are, an' should have some wit in your skull. Was that the way to carry on before the town, like a clown out of a circus? There isn't a neighbour doesn't know about it. Not one. An' the half of them think you're astray in the head. An' me took pride in you! . . ." For a moment her voice trembled, and the anger in her eyes was almost drowned, but she recovered herself. "When they told me first, I thought you were killed." Her voice hardened. "What do you think would have happened if the man had taken you at your word, an' had dropped you?"

Then Robert smiled. "There would have been a terrible mess on the floor," he said.

Her rage became unrestrained. The shock of the first rumour had torn her nerves to pieces, but she had contrived to keep control of herself until this piece of flippancy overthrew her. She lashed him with her tongue, while Margaret and Mattie and Alec stood dumbly by, too stunned by her wrath to speak. Robert listened until her rage was exhausted. The dark flush on his face had deepened as his mother reviled him until now he seemed like an Indian.

"Is that all you have to say?" he said, when she had done.

"No——"

"Well, it's all I'll listen to, then. I'm sick, sore an' tired of this house. Sick, sore an' tired of it, I am. You've talked to me as you wouldn't talk to a dog, an' I'm sick of it. I've tholed enough. I'll thole no more!"

Alec rose to restrain him. "Robert," he said severely, but Robert threw him aside. "Hell roast you," he said furiously; "leave me alone, you!" The oath rapped out of his mouth as explosively as if it were a shot from a gun, and the sound of it in that room, where oaths were never heard, was as terrible as blasphemy in a church. His mother rose at him.

"Go to your bed," she commanded.

"I'll go to no bed in this house," he replied, turning and running down the stairs to the shop. "I can't bear it or you either—you an' your family, the whole damn lot of yous!"

Margaret, who had tried to prevent him from leaving the room, went after him. "Robert, Robert!" she called to him, but he did not wait to answer her. They could hear the shop-door being opened and then violently slammed. For a moment there was deep silence. Then Margaret's sobbing came sounding up the stairs to them. They rose, Mrs. Dunwoody and Mattie and Alec, and made their way down to the shop.

"Open the door and call him back," Mrs. Dunwoody said, and Margaret, already struggling with the handle, did so.

They came out of the shop and stood in the dark street.

"There he is," said Alec, pointing to the figure of his brother who was running towards the bridge.

"Go after him," Mrs. Dunwoody said, her voice now very low and quiet. "Go after him, man, an' fetch him back!"

But Alec could not catch up with his brother and he returned alone and despondent.

"I called to him, but he wouldn't stop," he said.

"He'll come back in the mornin'," said his mother. "Come, daughter," she continued, turning to Margaret, who was crying by the fire; "come to your bed."

"I'll wait up for him," Alec said, "in case he comes back!"

"Do," said Mrs. Dunwoody.

THE FOURTH CHAPTER

I

HE could hear Alec's heavy steps behind him, as he ran over the bridge and along the Sand Quay, but he did not slacken his pace, even when Alec's panting entreaties to him to stop reached his ears. If Mattie or Margaret had followed him, he might have stopped, but Alec! . . . He felt a disgust for Alec rising within him. "The oul' Jenny-jo!" he said, and ran still harder. His brother's footsteps died away, and he knew that Alec was not pursuing him any longer. Alec was too short of breath to run much distance. "An' mebbe he's not so damned anxious to have me back," Robert thought. He was short of breath now himself, and he slowed down to a walking pace, and then, assuring himself that he was not followed, he stopped and rested. There were heaps of sand, red and brown and gray, lying on the quay, where it had been thrown from the lighters on the Lagan. He remembered that the lighter-men sometimes slept on their boats, and he wondered whether any of them were on board now. He might get a lie-down for the night. He stepped off the quay on to the deck of the nearest boat and listened at the top of the cabin-stairs, but could not hear any sound. A second lighter was moored alongside the first one, and he stepped across the gap between them, and explored it, too. It also was empty. He descended the

94

steps into the dark cabin, listening as he descended, and stood for a moment or two in the dark, as if waiting to be challenged, but nothing happened. He felt in his pocket for matches, but the box he carried was empty. He groped about the cabin, and then, suddenly overcome with fatigue, sank into a bunk and fell asleep.

It was still dark when he awoke, but he could hear footsteps above his head, and he realised that the lighter was no longer moored alongside the quay. He sat up, feeling cramped, and for a little while tried to sort out his thoughts. He had run away from home! That was the first and overwhelming thought in his mind. He did not know what the time was, but at least it was several hours since he had slammed the shop-door behind him and taken to the street. All this time, Mattie and Margaret and his mother and even Alec would be wondering where he was. Alec would probably have gone to the police-barracks and told the peelers about him! . . . He began to cry. He must have been crying before he realised what he was doing, for a tear suddenly splashed on his hand. He did not try to control his tears, but let them roll unchecked down his cheeks. He lay back again in the bunk, and listened to the slow, long steps of the lightermen as they walked along the deck, pressing the barge-poles into the bed of the river. At last, he had done what he had many times thought of doing; run away from home. He had shown his mother that he had a will of his own. Perhaps if he were to go back now, she would realise that he had a will of his own and not try to master him. . . . The morning light began to trickle into the cabin, and he sat up and looked about him. "It's not much of a place this!" he thought, and stood up. "Of course," he continued to himself, "it's only a lighter. I wonder where it's going!"

He had often leant on the parapet of the bridge, fascinated by the sight of the men pushing the long poles into the Lagan. He remembered how he had tried to propel a log as the lightermen propelled their boats. He had stepped onto the log, carrying a broomhandle with him, and had pushed off from the bank. Then he had thrust the handle down into the river and with difficulty had kept it firmly on the bed. But when he pressed his shoulders against the handle, as the lightermen pressed their shoulders against the poles, the log moved so swiftly that he could not recover himself and he fell into the water. He had realised then with what skill the lightermen moved their boats, and for a moment or two he dallied with the idea of taking a job on a barge. True, he had longed to go to sea and no one could say that a lighterman was a sea-faring man, since he travelled only on a river! Still, to start with! . . . He began to feel hungry, and as the light in the cabin was growing stronger, he went up the steps which led to the deck. His head emerged from the cabin as the lightermen were raising themselves from the poles and preparing to carry them to the other end of the deck where they would thrust them into the river again.

"That's a brave day," said Robert to them.

The lightermen looked at him. "What the hell are you doin' there?" one of them said.

He explained his position to them.

"So you've hooked it from home, have you?"

"Aye," said Robert.

"Well, you can just hook off this lighter as quick as

you like. Don't you run away with the notion that you're goin' to get us into trouble over the head of you——"

"I thought mebbe you'd give me a job."

"I'm more likely to give you a clout on the lug, comin' on board without as much as a word of permission. Get off to hell out of this!"

Robert glanced at the banks of the river, some distance off.

"How can I?" he said.

"You can jump ashore the way you jumped aboard! . . ."

The second lighterman made a suggestion.

"We'll land him at Molly Ward's," he said. "Then we'll not lose no time over the head of him!" They were late already, he said, adding to Robert that both of them had spent the night ashore in a celebration that had left them unsuitable companions for stowaways. At Molly Ward's locks on the Lagan Canal, Robert could step ashore, and find his way back to Belfast.

"Then you won't give me a job?" said Robert.

"Och, quit coddin' yourself!" the first lighterman replied.

II

They landed him at Molly Ward's, and he stood for a while with the lock-keeper, watching the lighter go through the locks into the canal. "Take my advice, young son," the second lighterman advised him, when the lighter was through, "go home to your ma like a good boy!"

"Aye, an' tell her to give you a skelpin' for stayin' out all night!" the first one added.

Robert, enraged by this, picked up a lump of earth and flung it in the first lighterman's face.

"You young get, you!" the man spluttered, spitting the earth out of his mouth.

"Mebbe that'll learn you civility," said Robert.

The lighterman was preparing to leap ashore. "Houl' that fella," he shouted to the lock-keeper, "houl' him 'til I bate the head off him!"

"Gw'on," said the lock-keeper to Robert. "Take to your heels, boy. That man's not accountable for himself when he's had a bellyful of drink, an' by the look of him he's had more nor he can houl'"

III

Again he was running away. Last night he had run from his mother and Alec. Now he was running from a drunken lighterman. But where was he running to? . . . He hurried along the Laganside, followed by the curses of the lighterman, and then slackened his pace to a walk when he realised that he was not being pursued. He was in a part of the town with which he was unfamiliar, for his life had been spent chiefly on the south side of the river. He had a rough notion of the district, but not an accurate one. The Botanic Gardens and Queen's College were near by. If he were to turn across these fields, he would probably reach the Malone Road, and then he would be all right; he could find his way home! . . . Home! He paused for a moment. What was he thinking about? He was not going home; he was running away from home. A nice object he would look if he were to go back now, running away for one night and then creeping home again!

Even Alec would mock him for that! No, he was not
going home. He did not know where he was going,
but this he knew, he was not going home. They could
say what they liked, he was not going to do that. And,
so resolving, he resumed his walk. The morning air
was very fresh and sweet, and he felt a sense of elation
as he crossed the fields. It was great value, this, to be
out in the early part of the day. He took off his boots
and stockings and walked barefoot through the dewy
grass. How delicious was the feel of the wet grass on
his feet! To walk like this was lovely, far finer than
paddling in the sea. Paddling bored him because it
made him feel as if his feet were bound. You strode
through the sea, with the water holding you, until you
were too tired to go on any longer. There was no
pleasure in that. But on dew-wet grass, you felt free.
You trod on it. The shining drops of dew flicked your
feet and legs as if they were trying to cool them. To
stand still and draw the sole of one of your feet up
and down a strip of glistening grass was unimaginably
pleasant. He had not noticed before how fine-looking
his feet were. His toes were thin and long and he
could almost grip the ground with them, they were so
flexible. The soles of his feet were red now, reddened
by the dew, and they had an extraordinarily clean look.
Feet, hitherto, had seemed ugly to him. He had always
averted his eyes when people stripped off their socks
or stockings in his presence, lest he should see their
ungainly feet; the ugly, discoloured nails; the big,
flabby toes, covered with corns; the unaired feet,
unpleasantly pale, the colour of lard. The boys and
girls who ran barefoot about the streets seemed to
have hides rather than skins. Their feet were hard

and always dirty. Sometimes they were sore! . . .
But his own feet, on this lovely, dewy morning, were
pink and shapely. He sat on a stone and rubbed his
hand along his wet legs until they were dry. Then
he wet his hands again with the grass! . . . There was
a singular sound of birds about his ears. The world
seemed to be silent, except for the great singing of
birds. For a moment or two he imagined that he was
alone in the world, that no other human being but
himself was alive, and that his ears would be regaled
by birds until he died. He stood up and looked about
him. High in the trees or hidden in the hedges, he
could see birds preening themselves or hopping from
branch to branch or twig to twig. How marvellous
that there should be so many birds in the world! Yet
how little he knew about any of them! He thought
that he knew what sparrows were—he called them
"spadgers" when his mother was not by to hear him—
but once he had been confounded by Paddy Kane who
had insisted, with the support of a man standing by,
that a flock of birds which Robert had called sparrows
were starlings. He knew what a blackbird was like,
and a thrush, but was uncertain about others. He would
like now to follow the length of the hedge, identifying
this bird and that bird, calling to it with its own note,
utterly confusing it by singing its song. Still, what did
it matter about names? Birds! That was name enough
for them. There they were, fluttering and flying and
twittering and cheeping, as happy as he was to be out
so early on that dewy day. If he could only see a nest
with eggs in it or maybe young ones! . . . Suddenly
he felt hungry and sticky and conscious of unbrushed
hair. He must somehow contrive to get a wash and

something to eat. He thrust his hands into the dew,
and then rubbed them on his face. He knelt on his
knees and hands and rubbed his face in the wet grass,
shutting his eyes as he did so. Then he stood up and
dried his face and hands on his handkerchief. A thrush
darted out of a hedge and flew close to him across the
field, chuckling as it flew, and he laughed, too. "I
don't know what you're laughin' at," he said, "but I
dare say you're right!" He tied the laces of his boots
together, and then swung his boots round his neck,
and walked on through the fields in the direction, as
he thought, of the Malone Road, but it was a long while
before he came to any road, and then he did not know
what road it was. He deliberated for a few minutes,
hoping that some one would appear who could direct
him towards the town, but no one did, and he continued his walk. He came presently to a field without a
gate through which he walked until he found himself
in the strangest place he had ever seen. He gazed
about him in astonishment, for the field had a singular
shape. It was made like a great horse-shoe; its grassy
banks seemed to have been built for spectators at some
sort of performance. In the middle of it was a heap
of stones, with a long heavy stone on top of them.
They seemed to have been set there. "You would near
think you were in a circus," he said to himself, as he
gazed about him. He walked in the centre of the
ring, and stood there, silent and unaccountably afraid.
In front of him, he could see the high, dark humps of
the Antrim Mountains, and seeing them, he realised
that he must have come away from the town when he
meant to go towards it. He was puzzled by the sense
of alarm he had. The field was a queer one, indeed,

but what was there to be afraid of? He moved away from the centre of the ring and climbed on to the bank and looked about him. That place over there, reaching out to the mountains, must be the Bog Meadows, where there was great skating in the wintertime. He had heard of them many times, but had never seen them before. And this place, what sort of a place was it at all? Who in the wide, earthly world would ever think of making a field this shape? Men had made it—of that he felt certain—unless it was like the Giant's Causeway that looked as if it had been made, but, according to all accounts, was not made at all. He walked round the ring until he found himself again at the place where he had entered the field. An old man approached him.

"That's a brave day!" Robert said.

The old man paused and looked at him. "Aye," he said, "it is!"

"What kind of a place is this at all?" Robert asked, turning to survey the field.

The old man gazed at him in astonishment. "D'you mane t'say you never heard tell of it?" he exclaimed incredulously.

"I wouldn't be askin' you about it if I had!"

"But you have the sound of a Belfast fella!" the old man persisted.

"That's just what I am—a Belfast fella. I was born in this place," said Robert.

"An' yit you never heard tell of the Giant's Ring! Well, man dear, that bates all I ever was toul'!"

"Is that what its name is? The Giant's Ring! Man dear! It's a queer-lookin' place!"

"Quare's the word for it! Quare, indeed! An' quare things happen in it!"

"What kind of queer things?"

The expression on the old man's face changed very quickly, from one of serene simplicity to one of cunning. "Oh, never mind," said he, nodding his head and turning away. "Never you bother your head. There's plenty of quare things a person might see, but he'd be the quare oul' gumph to go an' talk about them! There's things happen in that place that I wouldn't put a name til!"

"In the name of God, man, what kind of things are they?" Robert exclaimed, glancing fearfully at the Giant's Ring.

"Quare things!" the old man replied, turning down the corners of his mouth as if to signify that he would say no more.

"Bad things?" Robert asked.

"What d'you mane, bad things?"

"Well, fellas an' girls——"

The old man made a disdainful gesture. "Not at all!" he said. "Not at all! *Quare* things! Things that moidher your mind! In the oul', ancient days!"

"D'you mean ghosts?"

"Now, I'm not sayin' what I mane! You're young an' headstrong, an' you don't know the half mebbe that you think you know——"

"I never said anything about what I know!" Robert interrupted.

"Mebbe not, but there's a quare lot of hintin' in your talk, as if you were sayin' to yourself what a well-learned young fella you are, an' what an ignorant oul' man I am——"

"Sir," said Robert indignantly. "I never hinted nor thought any such a thing! I wouldn't be so lackin' in respect for you! I only asked out of curiosity!"

"Mebbe so, mebbe so," the old man replied in a mollified tone. "I'm not the one til take offence where none's meant, an' all I say to you is this, I wouldn't be in that place after it's dark this night or any other night, for a mint o' money. If the King of England was to come here on his bended knees an' say til me, 'John McClurg, I'll give you my crown an' my daughter an' all I have,' I wouldn't say 'Thank ye!' til him. I would not in sang! An' that's the last word you'll get out o' me, for I ought not til be talkin' about it at all! You don't know who's listenin' til you!"

He glanced nervously about him as he spoke, and Robert, himself slightly unnerved, glanced round, too. "There's nobody listenin' to you but me," he said.

"Och, man dear, have wit," McClurg exclaimed impatiently. "I'm not talkin' about people you can see!"

"Ghosts?" said John.

The old man became cautious and cunning again. "Now, name no names," he said, "an' make no remarks that could be took in a personal way. Some that might be mentioned, don't like bein' mentioned. An' anyway you never know how a person that's mentioned might take a remark. He might see a meanin' in it that was never intended, an' mebbe do somethin' til you that you'd sorely rue all your life. For there's more in that place, my young fella, than you can see on the grass, so take my advice an' mind yourself, an' don't be blather-skitin' roun' that Ring the way you would roun' the junction on a Saturday night! I'll lave you now, for I have work to do!"

"Thank you for your information," Robert said.

"Aw, not at all, not at all!" the old man murmured, as he moved away. He had not gone far when he turned back. "What I can't understand," he said, "is how you that's a Belfast fella don't know about it! Where in the world d'you live?"

"Over in Ballymacarrett!"

"Och, aye, that explains everything! Over in the County Down! Sure, the people over there knows nothin' at all! They're an ignorant lot! They have no rarin' at all!"

"They're as well reared in Down as they are in Antrim, an' mebbe a bit better, for there's the queer good blood in Down," Robert angrily retorted.

"Well, just as you say!" the old man remarked and turned away.

"Hi, wait a minute," Robert called after him.

"I can't stop here all day——"

"I'm not askin' you to stop all day! What's them stones for?" Robert pointed to the cromlech in the centre of the ring. A look of fear spread over the old man's face. "You have no wit at all," he said in a flickering voice. "No wit at all you haven't, to go on askin' questions like that! Be said by me, boy, an' go home like a good lad an' don't be standin' there annoyin' the oul' people——"

"Oul' people! What oul' people?"

"Did you never hear tell of the oul' ancient people?"

"There's been all sorts of oul' people in the world! What sort do you mean?" said Robert.

"The oul' sort that was here long ago. I forget the name they called them, but they were fearful people an' this place was where they come til say their prayers——"

"Druids, do you mean?" said Robert, hushing his voice.

"Aye, that was their name. Oh, dear, oh, dear, what

am I stan'in' here talkin' about them for, an' me with my work to do, an' them mebbe stan'in' listenin' til us!" He moved away from the field as quickly as he could, and when he had passed through the gate, he stopped and turned. "Come here, wee fella!" he said, almost in a whisper. "Come here till I'll tell you somethin'."

Robert followed him through the gate. "They call that place there a crumlick," he said, pointing to the cromlech. "An' it was on that big stone on the top that they offered up their sacrifices!"

"Sacrifices!"

"Aye, like the Jews did in the Oul' Testament! Only it wasn't sheep nor goats they offered up til their God, but people."

"Livin' people!"

"As livin' as you or me. Dead people was no use til their God! . . . D'you mind about Abraham and Isaac?" Robert nodded his head. "Like that," the old man continued, *"only they did it!"*

His hands were trembling as he spoke, and his face seemed drawn with fear.

"An' they're still doin' it," he said. "You never know when they'll come down the mountains an' across the Bog there, an' them mebbe havin' a young girl or a lad the like of yourself with them, an' when they get him or her there on top of that big stone! . . . Och, ochanee, what am I sayin' at all—me that has til live an' do my work here, an' them mebbe listenin' til every word I'm sayin'! Come away, son dear, an' not be annoyin' them!"

"Och, I'll just go an' have another wee look at the stones!" said Robert.

"Stones! Man, boy, them's not *stones!* Them's an altar!"

"Well, I'll have a look at it anyway!"

The old man did not stay to argue with him any more. He hurried along the lane, almost as if he feared that he was being followed. Robert looked after him until he was out of sight. "You oul' gomeril!" he said under his breath. "You an' your Druids an' your altars!" He returned to the field and walked to the centre of the Ring and stood by the cromlech. "If the half that oul' fella said was true," he thought, "there must have been queer carryin's-on in this place!"

He climbed on top of the cromlech and stood for a few moments surveying the scene. "What in the world will I do now?" he suddenly demanded. Then he laid himself down on the long topstone that stood at a strange angle to the other stones. "I'm just like one of the offerin's!" he said, and laughed aloud as he said it. His eyes were gazing at the blue sky above him. White balls of cloud rolled through it; lovely white balls of cloud that must, he thought, be full of snow. The sun shone on him, but was not yet strong enough to warm him. He could feel its rays on his face, and on his hands, when he folded them across his breast. If he were to lie there for an hour or two, he would soon be warm all over. . . . He closed his eyes, and lay very still for a few moments. Then he opened them again and stirred uneasily. He could not hear any sound. Birds had been singing when he climbed on to the stones, and he remembered hearing cattle lowing somewhere in the meadows. But there was no sound to be heard now. . . . He sat up and looked about him. The Ring looked as it had looked when he first came to

it. Nothing seemed to be different. But there was no
sound to be heard. He tried to stand up, but his feet
slipped from beneath him, and he fell flat on the big
heavy topstone, and suddenly fear seized him, and he
cried out, "Oh, Holy Christ!" He struggled on to his
side and fell off the stone on to the ground. Then he
scrambled to his feet and ran across the Ring to the
gate, while his heart violently thumped.

"Oh, Holy Christ!" he cried as he ran. "Oh, Holy
Christ!"

IV

He did not stop until he had run a long way down
the lane that led to the Ring. His heart was beating so
quickly that he put his hand to his side as if he were
trying to make it beat more slowly. Its swift beat hurt
him, and he sat down on a grassy ledge to rest. His
mouth felt parched, and he could scarcely breathe
because of the gulping in his throat. He looked about
him in a dazed way until the beating of his heart subsided and his breath came less pantingly. He felt sick,
and he lay back in the grass and closed his eyes. "You
dam' fool," he suddenly said aloud, "runnin' away like
that. Lettin' that oul' tow-wit make you feel afeard!"
He sat up and, after a moment or two, got on to his
feet. "Runnin' away from a lot of oul' stones!" He
turned and looked back towards the turn in the lane
which led to the Ring. "I'm near in the mind to go
back," he said, "an' lie down on it again just to show
I'm not afeard!" He paused for a few moments. "An'
I would, too, on'y I'm sore wi' hunger!"

He walked away, and presently came to a road where
a man directed him to Belfast. "I'll get myself some-

thin' to eat," he said, as he set himself towards the city.
He had forgotten his hunger, but now he was intensely
aware of it. His last meal had been his tea, taken before
he and Margaret had set out for the exhibition. The
quarrel with his mother had prevented him from getting
any supper. He had never been without food for so
long a time before. Fifteen hours! More than fifteen!
That was a long while! Well, men that went knocking
around the world were sometimes famishing for days.
This would be good practice for him! The queer thing
about his hunger was that it gave him no pain. He
had imagined that starving people suffered agony, but
his hunger was pleasant. He liked the sensation of
emptiness he had and listened to the odd rumbling noise
in his inside with a sort of delight. How he would
enjoy his breakfast when he got it! There was an
eating-place near the Town Hall, a round wooden hut,
standing by itself near the Morgue, and owned by the
Irish Temperance League. He would go there and
get a meal. Alec and he had gone there one time. They
had bought large cups of very hot coffee and big round
farls of soda-bread with sultanas in them. . . . He
would order that for his breakfast and a couple of
boiled eggs. Or mebbe fried eggs. If he had them
boiled, he could break them into a cup, with the yolk
and the white mixed up together, or if he had them
fried he could have ham with them. Two cups of
coffee and two eggs, fried or boiled, and mebbe a bap
or wheaten-bread. . . . His thoughts ran on food.
Would it be right to have a farl or treacle-bread—he
called it "trayckle-bread"—with ham and eggs? Or
would treacle-bread be too sweet? This was great value,
wondering what you would have to eat. When he

was younger, he had sometimes imagined himself alone
in a world full of shops. A long street of shops, all
stuffed with desirable things, mostly edible, stretched
from the top of the world to the bottom of it, and he
ate his way from one end of the world to the other. . . .
He felt in his pockets. The change from the half-
sovereign that his mother had given him so that he
might pay for admission for Margaret and himself to
the exhibition was still in his pocket. Eight shillings!
Many a man had faced the world with less! Anyhow,
he could afford to buy himself a good breakfast. He
hurried through the city, and, passing the Empire music-
hall and the Morgue, climbed a short flight of wooden
steps and entered the coffee-house. A man was sitting
at a table, eating sausages, and Robert, as he walked
past him, sniffed their savoury smell.

"Yes!" said the woman behind the counter.

"A cup of coffee and two sausages!" he said.

He ate the meal too quickly. He regretted that he
had not eaten the sausages very slowly and sipped the
coffee so that he might enjoy them for a longer while.
But it had been pleasant to fill his mouth with nearly
half a sausage and feel his teeth crunching through the
tasty mince. And the big draughts of coffee were delicious! Two cups of coffee he had drunk, two sausages
he had eaten, and a whole farl of wheaten-bread—for
there was no treacle-bread on sale! That was a good
breakfast, and he was almost in the mind to say his
thanks to God for it—only he was shy about praying
in public. When Alec and he came to this place to
tea, they had seen a Catholic girl crossing herself before
she began her meal. Robert had admired her for her
piety and had remarked to Alec that she seemed not to
know that anybody was looking at her. "Ah, they're

good people, the Papishes, about their religion!" said
Alec. "They're not a bit bashful about it!"

"I'll dare you to say your grace, Alec!" Robert
said then.

"That's no way to talk about religion!" Alec sternly
replied. "What kind of a spirit would that be—
thankin' God just for the cod of the thing! Ate your
tea, man, an' quit bletherin'!"

He rose from the table and walked to the counter
and paid for his breakfast. "Well, thank God, anyway,
for a good meal," he said, as he left the temperance
tavern. And now he had the day before him. What
should he do? Alec's shop was near by, and when he
recalled that fact, he felt a sudden, sharp desire to see
his brother. He walked towards Cromac Street, steadily
slackening his pace as he approached Alec's shop. This
was a queer thing to be doing! Anybody would think
he was trying to get back! . . . He halted in the doorway of a house opposite to the shop. Alec was not to
be seen, and Robert wondered if he might dart across
the street and peer through the window at him. He
made an excuse for what he could not deny was weakness. To be gaping into his brother's shop-window on
the very morning after he had abandoned his family
might be considered a sign of failing purpose. . . .
"But, sure, it's only natural," he said to himself, "to
want to see how he's takin' it."

He crossed the road, and peered into the window,
but could not see Alec because the interior of the shop
was dark. He was afraid lest Alec should come to the
door, and so he hurriedly re-crossed the street, and
stood again for a while in a doorway, hoping that his
brother would appear. But Alec did not come.

A boy passed by. "Hi, wee lad!" said Robert, taking

a halfpenny out of his pocket, "would you like to earn
a 'make'!"

"I would just," said the boy.

"D'ye see them buckets over there?" Robert continued, pointing to the pile of zinc pails which were
stacked by the door of the shop. The boy nodded.
"Well, I'll give you this 'make' if you'll go over and
cowp them!"

"What'll I do that for?"

"Och, never mind. Just cowp them an' run!"

The boy regarded Robert and then regarded the
buckets. "Is this a cod or what?" he demanded. "Are
you havin' me on?"

"I am not. I want to see the fella that keeps the
shop, an' I can't think of any other way of gettin' him
to come to the door! . . ."

"I'll do it for a 'wing,' " said the boy, bargaining
for a penny.

"You'll do it for a 'make' or you'll not do it at all."

The boy hesitated for a moment. "All right," he
said, "gimme the 'make' and I'll do it."

"If you don't," Robert replied as he gave him the
coin, "I'll follow you an' wring your neck for you!"

"You can trust me," said the boy.

He crossed the road and cautiously approached the
door of Alec's shop. He edged nearer and nearer to
the buckets, and then suddenly heaved them over and
ran away as fast as he could run. The clatter brought
Alec to the door. . . .

"He looks more upset about the buckets nor he does
about me," said Robert, as he sorrowfully turned away.

He wandered off, more miserable than he knew, and
presently found himself by the sheds in which the

cargoes from the cross-channel steamers were stored. If only he had enough money he could go to England or to Scotland. He walked along the quays, surveying the boats, and then sat for a long while on a stack of timber, while he gazed across the Lagan at the shipyard and listened to the incessant hammering of rivetters as they beat the sides of new ships together. He sat there until he felt hungry again, and then, after a meal at another temperance tavern, by a ferry, he lounged to the end of the harbour and stayed there until the dusk began to fall. A sense of solitude oppressed him, and he felt unaccountably sad and depressed. His eyes filled with tears. His courage was subsiding fast, and the audacity of his adventure had ceased to enthrall him. He wanted to go home. In the early morning, when the dew was on his bare feet, he had felt like a hero for whom the day could not be long enough, but now, after several hours of aimless wandering, after the sight of Alec patiently lifting up the pile of buckets and seemingly unconcerned about his brother, the day stretched too far in front of him. Time was too long. Evening would come, and night, and the next day and the day after. . . . His tears seemed to rise up from his heart. He could feel them flowing up through his body and filling his eyes. He could not see any more. The streets and the people in them were a wet blur. He wanted to go home again. Margaret and Mattie and his mother would be waiting for him . . . The figure of his mother appeared in his mind. He saw her tired, firm face and her fine eyes, full of love and reproach, and when, in his imagination, she turned to him and he saw how her heart was heavy with grief, he could no longer control his tears, and felt them flowing down his cheeks. "All right, ma!" he said aloud, "I'll come back!" The desire for adventure seemed to be dead in him. At that moment he was in the mood to do whatever his mother asked of him, to be a minister, to be anything she wished him to be. His love for her was now so wide and deep that he could not walk home quickly enough, and he began to run. Daylight had gone, and the darkness which lay upon the bridges was faintly lit by the yellow glare of gas-lamps. He stopped for a moment to recover his breath, and then hurried on again. Presently, the "Islandmen," as the workers at the shipyard were called, would come pouring through the streets in a great black mass, and he would be hindered on his way home. . . . He came to the corner of a dark and dingy street, running parallel with the Lagan, called Short Strand. If he were to go down it, he would avoid the "Islandmen" and delay. He hesitated for a few moments. The street and its miserable environs were mainly inhabited by Catholics of a rough class, and he feared to pass through it, after dark, lest he should be attacked. In one of the houses lived two idiot brothers whose heads were so tiny that each idiot was nicknamed "Johnnie Wee Head" or "Johnnie Pin Head." The imbeciles horrified him. Their horrible heads, that seemed to be no bigger than a man's clenched fist, filled him with a disgust that almost made him feel physically sick. If he were to meet one or both of them in the dark. . . . He shuddered, and almost turned away, but his impatience to be at home conquered his fear of the cretins, and he entered the street and walked by the wall of a timber mill. On the other side of the street were the mean

slum houses, and standing in the lit doorway of one
of them were both of the idiot brothers. Quite dis-
tinctly he could see them, their dreadful heads nodding
as they gabbled to each other! He stopped and shrank
into the shadow of a gateway, hoping that the sensation
of sickness which had come over him would quickly
pass. Then, when he felt that he had recovered, he
came out of the shadow still gazing apprehensively at
the imbeciles. One of them came away from the door
and peered at something behind Robert. He uttered a
yell, and came across the street, followed by his brother.
Terror overpowered Robert. He turned to go back by
the way he had come, and as he did so his arms were
seized, he was whirled round, and he saw a gang of
rough youths and heard a thick harsh voice shouting at
him, "Curse King William, you Protestant 'get' you!"
Then, because he did not reply, a fist suddenly struck
his face, and he could feel blood dribbling from his
nose. . [.] [.]

V

There were five lads in the gang which had seized
hold of Robert. One of them, with an evil face in which
little vicious eyes gleamed like the eyes of a rat, had
hold of his right arm and was twisting it so that he
felt it must presently be torn from its socket, while
another lad, undersized and sore-eyed, gripped his left
arm, pinching the flesh with his nails until it was sore.
The lad at his right arm seemed to be the leader of
the gang.

"Curse King William!" he shouted. "Go on, damn
ye, curse him!"

Robert did not speak. He shut his lips very tightly and tried not to cry with the pain he was suffering.

"Do you hear me spakin' to you?"

"I—I won't curse him," Robert moaned, and instantly the members of the gang gathered round him and beat him on the face and body with their fists. One of them kicked him on the shins, and the lad who had pinched his left arm began to pull his hair. He could not prevent himself from crying out with pain. "Oh, stop!" he cried.

"Well, curse him then!"

His lips trembled, and the tears filled his eyes. He paused for a moment while they stood around him, waiting for him to curse King William. Then he tightened his lips. . . .

"Are you not goin' to curse him?" the leader demanded, giving his arm a twist as he spoke.

"No!"

They pressed closely about him, thrusting his head back so that it seemed to him it must break away from his body. "Curse King William or I'll pull the bloody face off you!" the leader snarled.

Robert could not move or speak. They held him so tightly that only a gurgling sound came from his throat as he tried to say, "No, I won't curse him!" and the sound alarmed some of his tormentors.

"He's chokin'!" one of them exclaimed, hauling the leader away as he did so. They stood a few feet away from Robert, and watched him while he coughed and gasped.

"Have you had enough?" the leader demanded.

Robert put a hand to his mouth and nose and then withdrew it because his touch hurt him. There was blood on his fingers.

"I'll not curse him for you," he said with despairing courage.

They crowded round him again, pulling his hair and beating his skull with their knuckles.

"It'll be the best for you to curse him," one of them said.

"But I'll not curse him," said Robert.

He could see the vicious face of the leader of the gang turning more vicious still, and he shut his eyes and waited for the blow which he felt was coming—but it did not fall on him. He heard a shout, "Here's a 'peeler,' boys!" and suddenly the grip on his arms was released and he felt free. He opened his eyes and saw that the members of the clan, except the leader, were running away. The leader stood still for a second looking at the advancing policeman, and while he looked, resolution came into Robert's heart. He ran at him and gave him a violent kick, and fled, leaving the leader yelping with pain. And as he ran, he cried. His body shook with sobs. "They didn't fight fair," he said aloud. "They were afeard to fight me fair, though I wasn't their match. They'd no pluck! But I wouldn't give in to them. I wouldn't curse King William for them. I was too brave to give in to them. Wouldn't anybody else have give in to them except me? I know I was brave, for all the way I'm cryin' my eyes out!"

He turned and looked back to the scene of his torture. There were no signs of the clan. The policeman was standing gazing about him, but was not in the mood to make investigations.

"All the same," Robert said, still speaking aloud, "I'd 'a' been glad to give in to them—only I couldn't. I was heart-feared of them hittin' me, but I wanted to be brave more nor I wanted to give in, an' I couldn't let it be said the like of them made me do anything. Dirt, that's what they are! Just dirt!"

While he stood in the shadow of a church near the new bridge, stanching the flow of blood from his nose with his handkerchief, he heard himself addressed, and, turning round, saw Brenda Cairnduff and a girl whose name he did not know.

"Is that you, Darkie?" Brenda asked.

"It is!" he replied.

"I thought it was you, but I wasn't sure!" She hurriedly turned to her friend. "Well, good-night, Agnes! I'll not keep you——!"

"Oh, I'm in no hurry!" her friend answered.

"Well, I'll be a good while——!"

Her friend realised that Brenda wished to be left alone with Robert. "Good-night, then!" she said. "I'll see you Sunday!"

"On Sunday!" Brenda replied, as her friend walked away. "We've just come from a committee meeting in the church," she explained to Robert. "Oh, Darkie, whatever made you run away! Your mother's in a fearful state about you, and Alec never got a wink of sleep the whole night, sitting up for you, thinking, mebbe, you'd come back!"

"Oh!" he said sulkily. He had no wish to talk to Brenda then.

"Come on home now, like a good boy——!"

"I'll go home when I want to," he said.

He was still in the shadow of the church. She had not yet seen his bruised and bloody face. If only she would go away, he could slip across the street to where

the logs were lying in the Lagan, and dip his handkerchief in the water and wipe his face. . . . "Well, come
on with me!" she coaxed, putting her hand on his arm.
He turned as she spoke and the light of a lamp fell on
his face. She started back and uttered a little scream.
"Oh, Darkie, you've been fighting!" she wailed. "Your
face is covered with blood!"

"Mebbe you'll lave me now," he said sharply, turning
back to the shadow.

She stood for a moment or two irresolute and without
speaking. "I'm sorry I spoke to you," she said at
last. "I didn't dream you'd stoop to fighting in the
street——!"

"I didn't fight, I tell you. I was bate by Papishes
up there!"

"Oh, Darkie, I'm sorry!" She took hold of his arm
again.

"Och, lave me alone, can't you!" He shook himself
free from her. "I'm in no state to be seen——"

"Well, come with me, then, and I'll bathe your face
for you. We'll go down the back way and nobody'll
see you!"

He felt ashamed of his gruff abruptness. "Thank
you, Brenda," he said. "I'm sorry I was short with
you just then, but I couldn't help myself. Them fellas
gave me the quare hammerin', an' I was ashamed of
anybody seeing my face!"

"Never mind," she said, putting her arm in his.

She led him by dark streets to Modesty Row, in which
there was a gateway giving admission to the entry at
the back of the Terrace. "I'll see if it's open," she
said, but when she tried it, she found that it was bolted.

"Wait here a minute!" she said, "and I'll run into the house the front way and come out by the back and open it!"

He waited, as she bade him, and presently he heard the creaking sound of the rusty lock being withdrawn. They walked down the wet, earthy entry together until they came to the back door of Brenda's house. "It's lucky my mother's out!" she whispered to him. He glanced past her to where he could see the back door of his mother's shop. Here he was only a few yards from his home. Why was he bothering his head about Brenda when he had only to go a few steps down the entry and open a door and walk into his own home and be attended to by his mother? He hesitated for a few moments. Brenda moved nearer to him, and suddenly she began to laugh. He saw that she was looking across the entry to where the roof of the Salvation Army barracks could be seen rising above the wall. "D'you mind the time you fell through the roof and near frightened the drunk man out of his senses!" she said, pressing his arm in hers. He nodded his head. "You were always a desperate wee fellow!" she added, admiringly. He did not reply. He was wondering how much longer he could bear to remain here, talking to this girl, when his mother was only a moment's walk from him. "But you'll have to settle down some day, Darkie!" Brenda continued. "You can't go running wild all your life!"

How carefully she spoke. He glanced at her. Yes, she was nice-looking. Standing there in the dark, with her arm in his, talking in her genteel way, she looked nice. Only——

"Come in, now," she said, drawing him towards her.

"I put the kettle on the fire the minute I got into the kitchen, and it'll soon be boiling. Then I can bathe your face with nice warm water!"

He let himself be drawn towards her until they were standing close together.

"Kiss me, Darkie!" she said, putting her face up to his.

"My face is all blood!" he said.

"No matter!" she replied.

"All right, then!"

He kissed her, and she laid her head against his shoulder and seemed content to remain there. "Put your arms round me, Darkie!" she whispered.

"Hadn't we better go in?" he answered. "The kettle'll be boilin' over!"

She withdrew herself quickly from him. "Of course!" she said. "I was forgetting about your face!"

She led him into the kitchen and made him sit down by the fire. "Poor Darkie," she said, looking at his bruised mouth and nose. "They must have given you a fearful beating!"

"They did," he said, "but one of them'll bear the marks of me for a while. I hope I lamed him for life!"

"Aren't Papishes awful?" she murmured.

"Och, they're no worse than we are! I've seen one of them bate up the way I was!" He walked across the kitchen to where a small looking-glass hung on a wall. "Boys-a-boys!" he exclaimed, "but I look a sight to scare the world. I wonder you're not afeard of me, Brenda!"

"I'd never be afraid of you, Darkie, and I wouldn't care if I was!"

"Is the kettle boilin' yet?" he said abruptly.

She brought a tin basin into the kitchen and poured some of the hot water into it. "I'll make a cup of tea for you," she said, "when I've finished bathing your face!"

"I can do that myself——!"

"Let me do it, Darkie!"

She made him sit by the table, under the gas-light, so that she could more easily see what she was doing, and then very gently she sponged the blood off his face. "It doesn't look so bad, now!" she said. "It's a wee bit swollen, but that's all! Just dry yourself, will you, while I get you a cup of tea!"

"I don't want any tea, Brenda. I've given you too much trouble already!"

She turned to him quickly and smiled. "It's no trouble, Darkie!" They were silent for a moment or two, and then, as he dried his face on the towel she had given him, she said, "I expect you're starving with the hunger!"

"I am hungry," he admitted.

"It'll not take me long to make some toast for you!"

"Och, don't put yourself out on my account. Sure, I'll get something when I go in!"

But she did not pay any heed to him. She placed the toaster in front of the fire, and laid two slices of bread on it. "I dare say there's an egg in the house," she said, bustling into the scullery. He watched her, as she ran to and from the kitchen. "What are you thinking, Darkie?" she said.

"Nothing!" he answered.

But in his mind was the thought that she was nice-looking. Her movements were quick and sure, and when she turned suddenly, she turned gracefully. When

she knelt in front of the fire, he saw how slender her
ankles were. She had pretty legs! They sat down to
tea together. She had boiled two eggs for him and had
turned them into a cup and beaten them up for him.
There was a plate of hot buttered toast on the table.
The tea tasted good!

"You're quare an' kind, Brenda!" he said.

"Kind!" she exclaimed. "I'd do far more than that
for you, Darkie!"

"Why?" he demanded.

She hesitated. "I wonder at you asking such a question," she said.

He finished his tea and stood up. "I'll have to go
in now," he said.

"You're in no hurry," she answered. "Stay till my
mother comes home. She's up at my aunt's at Bally-
hackamore. She'll be greatly pleased to see you home
again!"

But he would not wait. "I ought to go in an' tell
my ma I've come home!" he said.

"Very well, Darkie!" she murmured, and then added,
"I'll come with you!"

She moved towards the hall, leading to the street-
door, but he did not follow her. "I'll go the back way,"
he said. She came back into the kitchen and stood
beside him. "Darkie," she said, "wouldn't it be nice
—wouldn't it be nice——!"

"Wouldn't what be nice?"

She glanced at the table where the remains of the
meal lay and then about the kitchen. "Oh, nothing!"
she said, and her voice was strangely altered. "Come
on!"

She opened the door that led to the yard, and he

followed her to the entry. They had to walk carefully now for there was no light and the ground was wet and dirty. "I'll take hold of your arm," she said.

"All right!" he replied.

"Listen, Darkie!"

"Listen to what?"

"Listen! I want to—no, it doesn't matter."

He laughed at her. "You're a quare one, Brenda," he said.

"Queer! What's queer about me?" Her voice had an angry note in it.

"Och, everything!" he said.

"I don't wonder the Papishes hit you," she said. "There are times when I could hit you myself!"

She turned and left him. "Aren't you comin' with me?" he said.

"No," she answered. "Good-night!"

"But wait a minute, Brenda——"

"Good-night!" she said, shutting the door. He heard the bolt being pushed into its socket. "Brenda!" he called, but she did not answer. Instead, he heard her steps as she walked across the yard, and, after a moment, the sound of the scullery-door being opened and closed again. He waited for a few moments, and then went down the entry to the back-door of his home. It was ajar, and he pushed it open and went into the yard. As he did so, Alec came out of a shed at the side.

"Who's that?" he called out.

"Me, Alec!" Robert replied.

"Oh, it's you, is it? So you've come home again— with your tail atween your legs!"

"I've not——!"

"Don't answer me, boy! I've had enough to thole through you! Up the whole night, waitin' an' watchin' for you, an' at my work all day. I'm sick, sore an' tired of your performances!"

Robert felt anger rising in him. "You didn't look so damned anxious about me when I saw you this mornin'," he said.

"This mornin'! When?" Alec demanded.

"When the wee fella cowped your buckets on you. I was standin' on the other side of the street!"

"You whelp, it was you set him on to cowp them!"

"I wanted to see you!"

"See me! Annoy me, that's what you wanted to do! Annoy me! God curse you, get out of my sight!"

"Where's my ma!"

"Where would she be? Tired out after searchin' the streets for you! But she could have spared herself the trouble! I knew rightly you'd come slinkin' home again! Get into the house there an' have done with your fool behaviour!"

"Are you orderin' me about, Alec!"

"Orderin'!" Alec came towards him, and even in the darkness Robert could see the anger in his eyes. "There's goin' to be a differs in this house in future, me fine fella! There's to be no more talk of makin' a minister of you or settin' you up with a fancy education. I've putt my foot down on that. You'll come intil the shop an' earn your livin' like the rest of us. An' the morra morn, you'll rise out of your bed an' go over til my shop and open it an' redd it out ready for me when I come over——!"

"Is that all you have to say, Alec?"

"All! No, nor the half of it——!"

"You can spare yourself the trouble of sayin' the rest, then! I'm not goin' to work in no shop!"

Alec seized him by the arm. "Go in," he shouted. "Go in an' go to your bed——!"

"Let go, Alec!"

"Go in, I tell you!" He tried to drag Robert towards the door that led into the shop, but Robert wrenched his arm away from him. "If you putt a finger on me," Robert said, "I'll break your jaw!"

"You that was goin' to run away break anybody's jaw! Come in, I tell you!"

Again he seized his brother's arm and tried to drag him indoors. "Hell roast you," Robert shouted, "let me go!"

Then, in his anger, Alec struck him in the face, and a fury suddenly filled Robert. "All right, then," he said, and, clenching his fists, he drove them, one after the other, full into Alec's face. Alec fell. "I've finished with you now," said Robert, as he left the yard. He ran along the entry until he reached the gate which gave on to the street. "I've finished with them all," he shouted aloud, as he opened it.

VI

He hurried through the dark streets, scarcely aware of what he was doing. He crossed the new bridge, and again found himself walking along the Sand Quay. Last night he had fled from his mother, Alec pursuing him, and now he was flying from his home again. Less than twenty-four hours had passed since he had hurried through this dark street, but he seemed to himself to have lived for years in that time. Was it only that morning that he had paddled his bare feet in the wet grass and had lain on the big stone in the Giant's Ring? When the birds sang to him—was that no longer ago than twelve hours? Already an age seemed to have passed since the corner-boys had beaten him in the Short Strand. Half an hour ago, he was sitting with Brenda! . . . Over there, behind the dark heaps of sand, the lighter, in which he had slept last night, had lain! And here he was again, angry and fugitive, not knowing where he was going or what to do! . . . He walked on until he reached the Queen's Bridge. He leant against the parapet and looked at the boats that would presently steam out to sea. Their hulls lay low in the Lagan, for they were loaded now and awaiting only the tide. He wondered if it would be easy to steal aboard a steamer and stowaway to England or to Scotland. If one were caught! . . . "Well, sure, they can't hing you for it!" he said, as he descended the steps that led down from the bridge to the harbour, and walked past the berths of the boats. There were men standing about the decks of several of the ships—he could not hope to get aboard one of them without being seen— but presently he came to a boat which seemed to be deserted. No one was on deck, no one was standing at the gangways, nor was any one loitering on the quay itself. If he were to run up that gangway now, no one would see him. He could hide himself somewhere. . . . He walked through an opening into the shed where the steamer's cargo was stored, and looked about him. A clerk was busy in an office, filling in lists. No one else was visible. He crossed the shed and looked into the street. Raindrops began to fall, as he stood there, debating with himself. Should he try it on?

Supposing he were to get away? He had scarcely any
money! He looked at the name in big letters at the
top of the shed. Glasgow. What would he do in
Glasgow? The rain dropped heavily now, and the
cold, wet wind made him shiver. Why could he not go
home? Aye, and face Alec with his jenny-jo ways!
. . . He turned quickly back to the shed, and stood
at the end of the gangway leading to the steerage.
It was quite safe for him to go aboard. No one was
about! . . . A great drop of rain fell on his hand as it
rested on the rail of the gangway, and again he shuddered. "It's terrible cold," he said, as he stole quietly
up the gangway on to the damp deck. He paused at
the head of a dark staircase and listened. No sound.
Then he went down the stairs and crept behind a
pile of stuff and slid down on the floor! . . . He must
have slept for a while, for presently, when the noise
of moving feet awoke him, he realised that the steamer
was about to sail. He could hear voices all about him,
and so, lest he should be discovered, he did not dare
to move, although he was cramped with lying in the
narrow, hard space in which he had hidden himself.
He must remain there until the morning and get ashore
somehow! . . . The syren sounded, and then he could
feel the ship throbbing as her engine moved. Voices
were calling above his head, and very clearly he could
hear people on the quayside singing a hymn to their
friends on board. He was on his way to Glasgow. It
was too late now to go back. The boat must be standing in the middle of the Lagan, preparing to move out
to the Lough and the open sea. Oh, God, what was
he doing here? Why was he running away like this?
. . . The ship's movements became swifter. Thump,

thump, thump, she went, as her propellers revolved more quickly. He lay in the dark and imagined each stage of the journey. They were passing the "Island" now, where the men on the night-shift would be hard at work. Now they were passing between the Twin Islands that made a channel at the mouth of the Lagan. The swifter movement of the boat showed that it had passed from the Lagan to the Lough. Presently, it would pass out to the Irish Sea! . . .

THE FIFTH CHAPTER

I

HE heard voices, and the sound of footsteps. Some one, several people, were approaching. They would find him and haul him in disgrace before the captain, who would order a sailor to rope-end him. . . . In the stories of stowaways that he had read, the captain nearly always had the shivering lad beaten with a hard, heavy rope and put to the roughest and most disagreeable work. The captain of this ship would not be able to set him to a long job, but he might have him arrested at Glasgow. That would be a poor performance, to be clapped into prison at the very start of his adventurous career! Perhaps if he were to move up a bit into the dark, he could keep himself concealed from the searchers for stowaways. It did not occur to him that the men whose voices he had heard were not searching for stowaways. It was the custom, according to the books, for a thorough search of every ship to be made soon after she left a port! He crawled along the narrow, dark space on his hands and knees until he felt certain that he could not easily be seen, and then, panting with anxiety and alarm, lay at down at full length. Stretched as he was on the deck in the dark, nobody was likely to see him. How he was to get off the boat undiscovered he did not know, nor did he dare to think about it. Probably he would be able to

slip off as easily as he had slipped on. He could tell a
few lies, if necessary. . . . Anyhow, it was of little
use to lie there and brood over what he must do in the
morning. He would try to sleep, and, making that
resolution, he turned over on his side and closed his
eyes. He had almost fallen asleep when he felt a hand
on his face, and he started up, striking his head against
a projection, and uttered a cry.

"Ssh!" said a voice that came from behind his head.
"Keep your mouth shut!"

"What is it? Who are you?" Robert whispered.

"I'm like yourself," the voice answered. "I'm gettin'
a free trip!"

Robert recovered his spirit. The presence of another
stowaway took some of his fear of discovery from him.

"Do you belong to Glasgow?" his companion asked.

"No, I belong to Belfast," he replied.

"Do you often do this?"

"Do what?"

"Get a free trip!"

"No," said Robert. "I've never been out of Ireland
before. This is the first time I've ever done this!"

He could hear movements, and presently saw the
other stowaway close beside him. "My name's Boak,"
the stranger said. "I've done this trip near a hunderd
times!"

"A hunderd times!" Robert exclaimed.

"Aye, backwards and forwards! An' never paid a
ha'penny for a trip. An' never was caught once!"
Robert listened to him in astonishment. "What do
you do it for?" he said.

"Ah, I just have a fancy for it!" he replied. "It's
great value!"

"I don't see it!" said Robert. "D'you mean to say you come back and from Belfast to Glasgow like this a hunderd times just for the cod of the thing!"

"That's right! But it wasn't always from Belfast to Glasgow. I've been a few whiles to Ardrossan——!"

"Holy God!"

"An' Liverpool an' places like that. But I've been to Glasgow the most times. I know it brave an' well!"

"What do you do it for?" Robert asked.

"Fun! I have an ambition to go a trip on every boat that sails from Belfast across the Channel, an' I've near realised it! I'll be back in Belfast the morra night—I mane to say I'll start from Glasgow the morra night!"

"On this boat?"

"Aye. I always like to make the return trip the way I went!"

Robert began to suspect that Boak was out of his mind, and he almost decided to creep out of his hiding-place and give himself up to the first sailor he met. After all, the captain could only rope-end him or give him in charge to the police, but this daftie sitting beside him in the dark might go stark, staring mad and do him an injury that would mark him for life. He began to crawl towards the opening.

"Lie still," Boak ordered. "D'you want them to hear you?"

"I only——!"

"Wheesht, wheesht, man! I'd be mortial offended if my record was broke through you. Lie still, an' be quiet!"

Robert subsided. Perhaps it would be better to humour the man.

"What notion took you to do this?" Boak presently asked.

"Oh, just the notion of an adventure. I wanted to see a bit of life!" Robert replied.

"What the hell's takin' you to Glasgow, then!"

"This was the only boat I could get on to without bein' seen!"

"Oh, aye! Were you ever in Glasgow afore?"

"I told you I was never out of Ireland 'til the night!"

"So you did!" Boak said. "Have you any notion of what you'll do when you get there?"

"I have not! Except mebbe get a job on a boat goin' roun' the worl' or somethin'! There's a lot of boats goes to places from Glasgow, isn't there?"

"Aha!" said Boak. "I believe they do, but I never had no fancy for that sort of a life myself!"

"You'd rather be doin' this!"

"Aye, I would."

Robert turned away. He felt no fear of Boak now. "Well, we all have our taste," he said, "an' God knows you seem to have yours!" He did not speak for a while, but when he remembered that Boak had boasted of having done the trip many times before, he turned to him again and said, "How'll I get off without any one seein' me?"

"Easy enough! They lift the tickets about now, an' all you have to do in the mornin' is to mingle in the crowd an' walk off!" Boak answered.

"But won't they be able to tell——?"

"Not at all! They'll be too busy berthin' the boat to bother their heads about anything else! You just do what I do, an' you'll be all right! What's your name?"

Robert told him. "Well, take my tip now an' lie down an' get a sleep. You'll be glad of it before the mornin' comes! Have you anythin' to rest your head on?"

"No!"

"Well, take this, then!"

He pushed something which seemed to collapse like a concertina across to Robert, who felt it and said, "What is it?"

"A life-belt," Boak replied. "Damned oncomfortable to lie on, but better nor nothin'!"

"Did you say you did this for fun!" Robert said, placing the life-belt under his head.

"I did!"

"You've a quare notion of fun," said Robert.

In the morning, Boak awakened him. "It's all right!" he said. "I've been up an' had a look roun'. There's a good wheen o' passengers aboard, an' we'll get off as easy as wink. You can come up on deck if you like!"

"Are we near in?" Robert asked, yawning heavily.

"We'll be in Glasgow in about a couple of hours. We're well up the Clyde now!"

Robert sat up. A faded sort of daylight dripped into his hiding-place. He felt sore and sleepy and slightly sick. His mouth had an unpleasant taste in it. "I'd give the world for a drop of tea!" he exclaimed.

"I'll get you a drop," Boak said. "Come on out now! There's a fella aboard makin' tay in the steerage an' he'll give you a drop. You'll have to drink it black."

"I'll drink it any way!"

"An' when you've had it, come up on top an' I'll show you the Clyde!"

Robert crawled out of his hiding-place and followed Boak into the steerage where a Scotsman was boiling tea in a tin can. "D'ye think you could spare a drop for this chap?" Boak said to the Scotsman, who murmured, "Oh, aye," and poured out a cupful of the hot, black, sugarless tea. Robert greedily swallowed it although it burnt his throat. "Would you like a drop more?" the Scotsman asked.

"Thank you!" said Robert, holding the cup out to be filled.

"Tay puts heart intil you," Boak said.

He held up the cup as if it were a glass containing wine. "It's the national drink of Irelan'!" he said. "Many's a time when I was coul' an' wet an' sick an' sore, I just put the kettle on the coals an' boiled myself a cup o' tay, an' in a wee while I felt as right as rain! Man, dear, but God was in the quare good form the day He made tay!" He drank his tea almost at a single draught and seemed not to be affected by its hotness. "Come up on top," he said to Robert, "an' take a look at the country roun' the Clyde! It's a great place!"

Robert held back. "But is it safe?" he said.

"Safe enough," was the answer. "Anything's safe if you're not afeard of it! I foun' out long ago that the fella that's always safeguardin' himself is the one that gets intil all the trouble! If you look as if you had a right to be where you are, people'll think you *have* a right!"

"Mebbe he's not such a daftie as I thought," Robert said to himself as he followed Boak up to the deck.

"Just mingle with the crowd an' don't draw attention to yourself," Boak whispered, as they reached the top of the steerage stairs. "It's a misty mornin' an' you'll never be noticed!"

Gray clouds cast gray reflections on a gray sea, and a cold wind, that seemed to be as gray as the sea and the sky, blew bleakly across the Clyde from the Mull of Kintyre. Behind him, almost hidden by mist, was the island of Arran, and in front of him was narrowing water with wet-looking hills on one side and sombre fields on the other. He shivered as the wind blew about him.

"You should 'a' brought a big coat wi' you," said Boak.

"I didn't think of it," Robert replied. "Where are we?"

"Them's the Highlands startin' over there," Boak answered. "Man, boy, but you should see them hills on a clear day, wi' the sun shinin' on them. Gran', that's what they are! Many's a time I've stud here of a summer mornin' an' lukked at them. D'ye mind that wee bit in the Bible, how does it go now? Oh, aye! It comes in Isaiah!" He raised his head and almost shouted the verse. "For ye shall go out with joy, and be led forth with peace: the mountains and the hills shall break forth before you into singing, and all the trees of the fields shall clap their hands." He turned to Robert when he had finished and said, "An' I declare to my God there's been times when I saw them doin' it!" He was silent for a few moments while he looked about him. The flat coast of Ayr was rising up to low headlands, and the deeply-indented shores of

Argyle rose swiftly up to the mist-drenched mountains. White gleams of sunshine shot across the smoky-gray clouds and tried to burn up the mist, but they were not warm enough, and they wavered weakly on the sea. Steamships and sailing-boats drifted up and down the Clyde, and now, as the land closed in, Robert could see signs of human life. He was terribly cold and terribly hungry. He had had nothing to eat since Brenda had given him the cupped eggs and toast, and when he thought of buying food, he felt frightened, for he remembered how little money he had. But what was the use of making a poor mouth of himself? Plenty of people had started off with no money at all! . . . His reflections were interrupted by the voice of Boak, and he turned to listen to his companion. Boak was older than he had first imagined him to be. His face was thin and deeply lined, and his untidy, straggling hair was patched with gray. The wind had stung his eyes and reddened them and made them water, but there was light left in them, and it made them glisten. "When I see them hills," he was saying, "standin' there in the sun, an' all the colours of the rainbow shinin' on them, an' I feel the spray blowin' off the sea and wettin' my face, I feel quarely satisfied for all the sorrow an' discomfort of this world!"

He began to hum under his breath.

"Wheesht!" said Robert, fearful lest attention should be drawn to them.

"Wheesht what?" Boak demanded.

"Quit singin', man! Somebody'll hear you!"

"What odds if they do!" And he began to sing aloud:—

> "All people that on earth do dwell,
> Sing to the Lord with cheerful voice,
> Him serve with fear, His praise forth tell,
> Come ye before Him and rejoice."

"Listen!" said Robert, taking hold of his arm. "It's a quare thing that a man so religious as yourself should take trips on boats without payin' your fare!"

Boak ceased to sing. "It is quare," he said, "but I daresay God'll forgive me on the Judgment Day when He sees the way I appreciated His worl'!" He resumed his singing without a pause:—

> "Know that the Lord is God indeed,
> Without our aid He did us make,
> We are His flock, He doth us feed,
> And for His sheep He doth us take."

"Well, if it's a meetin' you're going to hold, I'll go down below again," said Robert.

Boak seized him by the arm. "Wait! Wait, man!" he said. "Wait 'til you come roun' that corner there!" He pointed to where the Clyde sharply bent to the east and turned round the corner of Renfrewshire. "Wait 'til you see the grandeur of God starin' you in the face, and then mebbe you'll want til sing, too!"

The ship turned the corner and moved past Greenock and Gourock. "Look there!" Boak exclaimed, pointing over the river to where Loch Long and Gareloch ran up into the highlands of Dumbarton. "Isn't it wonderful to· see them all spreadin' our fornenst you like that, wee hills an' big hills an' deep water." A religious fervour seemed to possess him, and he walked to the side of the ship, dragging Robert with him, and while he gazed on the beautiful country that lay before them, he began to chant: "I will lift mine eyes to the hills, from whence cometh my help! . . ."

Suddenly he broke off. The light died out of his dimmed eyes, and fear came in its place. He shut his eyes and began to pray. "Oh, Almighty an' everlastin' God!" he said in a quavering voice, "whatever I do against You, an' whatever You do to me, don't putt me where I'll never see Your hills and mountains no more. For Jesus Christ, His sake, Amen!"

He relaxed his hold on Robert's arm, and stood with his hands on the rail. "Wonderful God!" he murmured aloud. "Wonderful! You done well, God, You done well!"

Robert looked anxiously around. Two sailors were standing a little way off, regarding them with curiosity, and he feared that they knew that he and Boak were stowaways and would presently arrest them. He moved away, leaving Boak to contemplate the hills. One of the sailors followed him, and so, feeling that it was useless to try to evade him, Robert stopped and waited.

"Was Boak botherin' you?" the sailor said.

"No! Oh, no!" Robert replied, made more nervous on hearing Boak's name mentioned.

"Don't let him upset you! He's a harmless fella! Mad! Stark, starin' mad!"

"D'you know him, then?" said Robert.

"Know him! As well as I know myself. He's travelled this trip a score o' times an' more, an' he thinks nobody knows he's a stowaway, but we know right enough! The poor fella's astray in the head. Was he talkin' to you about mountains?" Robert nodded his head. "I thought so. He has mountains on the brain! Don't let him bother you!"

Robert realised that although Boak was known to be a stowaway, he was not. "Thank you," he said, going down the stairs to the steerage, "I won't."

II

When the ship berthed at Jamaica Bridge in Broomielaw, Robert edged himself well into the crowd and hurried as quickly as he could across the gangway. Boak was close to him, and seemed to wish to stay near to him, but Robert did not desire to spend any more time in his company, and so he eluded him on the quay. His recollections of the imbecile brothers of the Short Strand were too recent and miserable for him to be willing to associate with another daftie, although Boak's ecstacy over mountains queerly attracted him. He walked away from the quay with no notion in his head of what he should do. If this was Glasgow, then he could see no point in leaving Belfast. Dreary, dribbling streets of high houses, bare as barracks, strained away from the river, and hordes of dishevelled children, all with noses in need of attention, squalled about the wet pavements. The painted fronts of the gaunt, flat-faced tenements were peeling, and pieces of sodden paper stuck to the doorsteps. He stood for a few moments in a doorway to shelter from the rain which fell dirtily down through sheets of smoke, and glanced about him. On the opposite side of the street was an eating-house that had a look of steamy comfort, and he ran across to it and sat down at a marble-topped table which was still damp from the careless wiping it had received from a big, red-faced, thick-wristed girl who was slopping a wet cloth along the counter. The shop smelt of stale air and hot fat and innumerable meals, and everything that he touched was slimily wet. The slattern behind the counter had not washed away the grease on the tables, but had merely dribbled water over it and wiped some of the water away. The sticky débris of many meals seemed to be mingled with the sawdust on the floor, and Robert, fresh from the sea, felt himself turning sick in the fœtid atmosphere. He rose from the form on which he had seated himself, but before he could turn towards the street-door, the girl called to him, in a thick voice, "Did ye want your breakfast?"

"Are you Irish?" he said.

"Me father an' mother are Irish," she replied. "I'm Scotch!"

She came from behind the counter as she spoke, and stood beside the table at which he had again seated himself. "What'll I get you?" she said.

He had not the courage to tell her that all he now wanted was to get out of the stinking shop, and so he ordered tea—"as hot as you can make it"—and bacon and eggs, and ate them as quickly as he could.

"Are you Scotch?" she said, as he paid for the meal.

"No," he replied, "I'm Irish!"

"Irish, are you? You talk like a Scotchman!"

"I come from Belfast! . . ."

"Ah, the Black North," she interrupted. "My father and mother come from Cork!"

"I daresay," said he, picking up his change, "but I come from the civilised part of Ireland!"

He left the shop before she had time to speak her mind to him and hurried through the rain in the hope that soon he would come to the centre of the city. He was nearer to it than he realised, and presently he found himself outside a public library. The rain still fell, and, overcoatless as he was, he feared that his clothes would soon be sodden. He could shelter in the library, and, perhaps, find information about work in the newspapers. He must quickly get employment. He might have to wait a long time before he got a job on a ship, and work of some sort to keep him alive until that time was needed. He had no clothes but those in which he stood up, and he could not go to sea without a kit. . . . There was a group of men standing in front of each of the newspapers on the stands, and when at last he succeeded in getting near enough to the *Glasgow Herald* to be able to read the "Wanted" advertisements, he found nothing among them that was likely to suit him. He wandered into the magazine room, and sat down at a table covered with reviews, and turned over the pages of *The Nineteenth Century*. He must think and think hard. So far his adventure had been a poor, profitless thing. He was wet and cold and presently he would be hungry again. . . . Food suddenly became a menace to him. The regularity with which it was needed now seemed to be a calamity. If a man could do without meals! . . . He had better be careful with his money. Hitherto he had bought a meal for himself immediately he felt in need of one, but that sort of conduct would not do at all. He must make each meal last longer. Perhaps he could skip a meal. If he were to go without his dinner to-day and eat a good tea! . . . Starvation had no attraction for him. Adventurous men often had to go without food, sometimes for days, and their bodies might be reduced to skin and bone, but he had never

heard or read that they *liked* starvation.   And there
was the question of lodgings.   He would have to sleep
somewhere that night.   But where!   The money he had
would not keep him in food for long; it would soon
be spent if he had to pay for a bed as well.   He must
get work!   If only there were a ship waiting for him!
He walked to one of the windows of the library and
looked into the street.   The rain had ceased to fall,
though the pavements were still very wet.   If he were
to walk about the streets for a while, he might find
something to do—anything—even if it were only to
carry a bag or push a barrow! . . . His pride was
terribly wounded when he thought of himself carrying
a bag, but his urgent need to earn money made him
ignore the wound.   There was a railway station somewhere near the library; he remembered to have seen
it as he ran through the rain.   He might pick up a
few pence there and hear of a place in which to stay
for the night!   He left the library and asked a man in
the street where the station was.   "What station do you
want?" the man replied.

"The nearest one!" Robert said.

"Then Central's the nearest, but St. Enoch's isn't
far off!   Where do you want to go?"

"I don't want to go anywhere.   I thought mebbe
I'd get a job or two! . . ."

"Oh, you're out of work!   Well, I'm sorry for you.
The Central's just round the street here.   I daresay
you'll do better there than anywhere, though there's
not many people in this city needs to have their bags
carried.   They generally carry them themselves!"   The
man hesitated for a moment.   "Mebbe," he continued,
"you'd let me lend you a shilling! . . ."

He offered the coin to Robert as if he were afraid
it might be refused. "Oh, thank you, sir," Robert
said, taking it from him. "But I've done nothin' for
you!"

"Och, well, mebbe you will some day, and if you
don't do anything for me, well, perhaps, you'll be able
to do it for somebody else. You look a very well-reared
young fellow! I'm wonderin' what's brought you to
this!" Robert didn't reply. "Have you run away?"
the man asked. Robert nodded his head. "Well,
take my advice, and run home again!" said the man.
"Good-day to you!"

"Thank you, sir!" said Robert.

III

He became tired of hanging about the Central Station when after three hours of hard competition with
other would-be bag-carriers, he found he had earned
twopence, and so he wandered aimlessly off. He had
eaten nothing since his early morning breakfast, and
although he felt very hungry, he was resolved that he
would not eat until late in the evening. By walking
about the city he could keep his mind off his hunger!
. . . These streets were full of people, but he knew
none of them. There was no one person in the great,
dripping city from whom he could claim friendship.
He was terribly alone in all this company of people.
Even the man who had so suddenly and unexpectedly
given him a shilling was only a kindly memory of a
kindly stranger. At home, now, he could scarcely walk
through the streets without meeting some one with
whom he was acquainted or familiar. But he had left

all that friendliness and was now committed to wandering and solitude for the rest of his life—for he could not go home again. He could not return to his family and confess himself a failure, disheartened by homesickness! . . . Oh, God, how homesick he was! His thought continually recurred to familiar things, little, common, dull things that were not worth a thought, but now seemed extraordinarily interesting and important: the smell of the wind blowing up the Lagan from the Lough or across the city from the hills; the gleam of lamplight through a blue blind; the sound of an Ulster voice; the way in which his mother's face would suddenly relent and a fragrant smile would replace the severity of her look; Mattie's pretty face and Margaret's quick, running laugh; Alec's silly, dribbling, unbalanced moustache! . . . If Alec were to appear before him now, he could almost find it in his heart to hug him. It was queer that Alec and he never got on together. Alec always seemed to be jealous of him, kept on hinting about favouritism! . . . Perhaps Alec *was* jealous of him. That would account for much in their lives! . . . Well, he would have no cause now for jealousy. He would be the only man at home in the future, and there would be no Robert with whom to share his mother's love! . . . That dismal thought made his eyes fill with tears, and he stopped and leant on the parapet of a bridge over which he was crossing until the blur had faded from them. This, he supposed, was the Clyde! Well, give him the Lagan any day! He stood, with his arms on the bridge and stared down on the muddy water beneath him. It was not any muddier-looking than the Lagan, really, only . . . !

"Och, to hell!" he said, aloud, turning away from

the parapet and walking towards the south side of the river, "what's the good of broodin' like this! I've run away, an' that's all about it! If a fella runs away from home he should run away an' not stan' about the streets frettin' an' makin' a poor mouth of himself. I'll think no more about things! I'll try an' get aboard a boat an' go roun' the world or somewhere——!"

He hurried across the bridge and presently found himself wandering through still drearier streets than those in which he had wandered during the early part of the day. "Be rights," he suddenly said to himself, "I ought to send a postcard home to say I'm safe an' soun'—just to keep them from frettin' about me!" But that might be taken in the wrong way, as a sign of weakness, a signal of distress. No, he would not send a postcard, not yet anyway! . . . He turned a corner, and found himself in a street which ran across a tract of black, barren-looking land. There were no houses at this end of the street, but on one side of it was a broken paling through which he caught sight of some factories and a wide tract of earth, pitted with deep holes or heaped with factory rubbish. There was an open gateway in the middle of the paling, and he stood in it for a while and surveyed the dismal scene. A brick-kiln stood on the left of the gate, and as he looked at it he saw labourers wheeling bricks from doorways in the kiln. In front of him were deep pits where men were filling barrows with clay. Heaped above these pits were great piles of slag thrown there from the furnaces of the workshops that stretched away on his right as far as he could see. He picked his way across the slippery ground, full of puddles, and stood on the edge of one of the clay-pits; a great, wide,

deep hole, with slime and stagnant green water at its
bottom, and a long slide of white dust and slag spilling
down one side of it like a running sore. Here and
there in the heap were odd-shaped pieces of slag, some
of them still whole, some of them broken, that seemed
to have been taken from a mould. Robert stared down
at the green puddle at the bottom of the pit and then
up at the dark gray sky, growing grayer and darker,
and felt the damp, cold wind blowing into his bones.
Hell must be like this! Perhaps the damned spent
eternity filling barrows in a hole like that! . . . It
seemed impossible that the earth could ever be made
to look so foul. He remembered the dewy fields outside Belfast through which he had walked barefooted
—when? Only two mornings ago! And the Giant's
Ring and the Bog Meadows spreading greenly to the
mountains! This obscene place must once have been
like them. He stared about him, as if he were stunned
by all the ugliness he saw. At one edge of the defiled
ground he saw a row of tall houses that looked across
this dreadful place to the brick-kilns and the workshops
and the furnaces. Out of those windows, people gazed
upon this desolation! . . . He walked towards the
brick-kiln, and stood at one of the entrances and
watched the men wheeling the dried bricks into the
open. The hot air flowing from the kiln warmed him.

"Would I be let in there?" he said to one of the
workmen.

"Go in if you want to," the man replied. "There's
two others in there now!"

"Two others?"

"Aye, a couple like yourself, I suppose, out of work
an' down on their luck! Go in and warm yourself!"

Robert entered the warm kiln, and stood in the centre of it. There were two elderly men sitting on a bench at the side of it, one of whom seemed to have innumerable pieces of paper on his knees.

"Sit down there, if you want a rest," said the workman. "Nobody'll disturb you while we're workin' here!"

Robert did not speak, but sat down on the bench beside one of the tramps. He was so tired! . . .

The tramp with the pieces of paper did not speak to him. He folded and unfolded and folded again his pieces of brown paper and newspaper, as if they were extraordinarily precious to him. He seemed to be unaware of the workmen or the other tramp. Occasionally he muttered words to himself that sounded meaningless to Robert. One phrase he repeated several times. "Goin's-on," he said, "everywhere!" Robert leant back against the wall, and as he did so caught the eye of the second tramp who touched his head and then pointed at the tramp with the pieces of paper. "Come far, mate?" he said.

"Belfast," Robert replied.

"Ireland, eh! I come from London meself. Been 'ere before?" Robert shook his head. "Not a bad doss, if the cops 'ud leave you alone!"

"Cops!"

"Yus. Can't leave you alone! Come in 'ere sometimes an' shifts the lot of us aht! Can't leave us alone!"

A workman, wheeling a barrow of bricks into the open, overheard his complaint. "Well," he said, "you know why that is. You chaps have no respect for a place, an' it's no' sanitary to let you alone! You'd hae this place in a fearfu' condeetion if the police didnae shift you frae it. Epideemics, mebbe!"

"Well, 'ow can we 'elp ourselves! There ain't no modern conveniences abaht, are there? I ain't nowticed no plumbin' or sanitary enginecrin' any'ow, an' the Scotch ain't so blasted partic'ler neither!"

But the workman had gone without waiting to hear the tramp's reply. Robert, his eyes now accustomed to the gloomy light in the kiln, gazed about him. Piles of bricks were all about him, some no more than blocks of wet, shaped, dark-brown clay, some newly baked into bricks, others quite hard. The ground was covered with a thick brown powder, where the clay had dried into dust. A gentle draught of warm air permeated the kiln, flowing from chamber to chamber, and Robert felt himself soothed by it. His head relaxed, his eyes closed. In a few moments he was asleep.

IV

He felt himself being violently shaken, and he started up shouting, "What is it, Alec?" Then he remembered that he was not at home, asleep in the attic with his brother, but a runaway asleep in a brick-kiln in the company of tramps. An unfriendly voice was ordering him to get up and get out, and a jet of light was streaming into his eyes. He looked up and saw a policeman bending over him. "Come on," he was saying, "you can't sleep here!" He stood up, half stupid with sleep and fatigue and blinked his eyes. The tramps had gone, and the policeman was impatient for Robert to be gone, too. "Out you get," he said, "an' if I catch you in here again to-night, I'll arrest you!" Robert did not answer, but walked towards the entrance to the kiln. As he came out of the kiln, the cold air sent shivers through his body. He felt chilled to the spine.

"It's terrible cold!" he said to the policeman, who was at his heels.

The policeman glanced at him sharply. "You seem a decent lad," he said. "What brought you to this?"

"Want!" Robert abruptly replied.

"Want!" the policeman repeated. "Have you no home or friends?"

"Not now!"

"Well, it's no business of mine, but I don't like to see a lad like you sleepin' wi' tramps in a brick-kiln——"

"Can't I stop here 'til the mornin'!" Robert pleaded.

"I'm sorry. You can't. The people that owns the place has had to complain about tramps sleepin' here. They've no respect for it——"

Robert nodded his head. "I know," he said. "I heard about it. What's the time?"

"Nearly ten o'clock!" the policeman replied.

Ten o'clock! He must have been asleep for hours! And without food! He had had nothing to eat since breakfast time and he felt as if he were empty.

"Well!" the policeman said loudly.

"All right, constable, I'm goin'!"

"Sorry, boy, but you've got to suffer for the others!"

Robert stumbled out of the kiln, shivering with the cold, and walked towards the broken gateway through which he had entered earlier in the evening. As he passed the corner of the kiln, he heard himself called.

"Hist!" the voice said. "Hist, hist! Is the cop still there?"

"Yes," Robert answered, recognising the voice of the tramp who had spoken to him in the kiln.

"Blast 'im!"

Robert went on towards the gate.

"W'ere you goin'?" the tramp said.

"I don't know," Robert answered.

"Wait a minute!"

He stopped and turned and waited until the tramp came up to him. "No good goin' back there!" he said. " 'E'll run you in the clink if 'e catches you there again! Better come along o' me!"

"Where?"

"Over 'ere!" He jerked his thumb towards the slag-heaps behind him. Robert looked across the dark space where he had seen the clay-pits.

"There?" he said.

"Yus! Git a bit of a warm, any'ow! Better'n nothink any'ow! Come on!"

He moved into the darkness, and Robert followed him. "Be careful 'ow you tread," the tramp said. "This blasted 'eath is full of 'oles, an' you might fall a nell of a long way into a stinkin' puddle an' get drahned! Keep close to me, an' you'll be all right!"

"Where are we goin'?" Robert asked.

"Up one of these blasted slag-'eaps," was the answer he received. "Mind 'ow you step!"

They were walking on the edge of the deep pit from which he had seen the workmen drawing the clay, and presently they reached the first of the great hills of ashes and white dust that had risen up from the waste-land, made out of masses of hot slag, drawn from the iron-works and dumped here. Robert remembered that he had seen the big "pugs" of slag, some of them still red from the furnaces and weighing several tons, tipped out of the trucks on to the heap. One of them had rolled down the side of the hill into the slimy green water at the bottom, where the rains had collected and made a foul lake, and had been submerged under the steam and bubbles. He had thought to himself then how deep that dark green pool must be, and now he shuddered with fear lest he, too, might go tumbling down into its depths. Even in the darkness he could see the "pugs" standing lop-sidedly on the slag-heaps like old tombstones in a neglected graveyard, and he thought to himself that this place might be a cemetery in hell, in which the utterly damned were buried. There was a "pug" above him which seemed to be so lightly poised that a touch might send it reeling down to the pool. The tramp was toiling towards it. Robert paused to straighten himself. The air was full of rain and sleet that drenched him to the skin, and a bitter wind pierced his dripping clothes and cut his flesh. Great red and orange flames flared from the chimneys of the iron-works and made a brief and flickering illumination on the slag-heaps and the clay-pits and the white "pugs" and the green pool and the mud and puddles of the waste-land, but there was no other light, for heavy, black clouds scudded across the sky and concealed the moon.

"Well, it's no good grum'lin'!" he said to himself. "I asked for it, an' I've got it!"

He followed after the tramp, stumbling now and then in holes in the ground and once his foot went into a puddle of rancid water that had somehow failed to find its way down to the pool. There seemed to be

no one but the tramp and himself alive in this dank
world of clay and ashes, and for a melancholy moment
he imagined that mankind had perished, that the earth
had been consumed, that presently he and the tramp
would turn to a heap of white dust and cinders and
drift down to the pool and be buried in green slime!
. . . His thoughts were suddenly dispelled when his
foot caught in something soft that was half-covered
with the warm white dust and he fell forward on his
hands and face, scraping them on cinders. A horrible
fear filled him as he fell, for he had felt the soft thing
yield as he trod on it, and he wanted to get up and run
away even if he fell into the pool in his flight. But his
fear left him when he heard himself cursed and reviled
and he turned and saw that a tousled head was emerg-
ing from a heap of rags with which its owner had
covered himself after he had dug into the warm ash.
Presently other heads were lifted, and Robert saw that
he was surrounded by men who had nearly buried
themselves in the slag. As they sat up in the white ash
and let the rain dribble in dirty streaks down their
dusty cheeks, it seemed to Robert that the grave was
giving up its dreadful dead. On some horrible battle-
field corrupting men must lie about in heaps as these
men lay on that hill of slag. The rain and sleet still
fell and the bitter wind still blew, but he no longer
felt them, for the air was warm and seemed to be
getting warmer! . . . Perhaps he had died in his sleep
in the brick-kiln and his damned soul was now
meandering along the first slopes of hell. Those red
and orange flames that splashed across the black sky
and turned the green pool to a copper colour came
from infernal fires. He was dead and damned! . . .

The tramp's voice called to him again. "Over 'ere," it said. "A bit of all right, it is!"

He glanced fearfully about him and saw that the men he had disturbed were wriggling back into the holes they had made for themselves. "Like rats!" he thought. In a few moments they were still again, and the darkness covered them; he could scarcely see them, so closely had they assimilated themselves to the slag, and he wondered, in his weakness, for he felt faint with hunger, whether he had imagined their presence. Phantoms! Phantoms that crept out of the ground and cursed horribly and crept back again! . . .

"'Ere, cahm on!" the tramp called to him in a fretful voice. "Blimey, you down't 'alf tike a time!"

"Where are you?" Robert replied.

"'Ere!"

He could see the figure of the tramp further up the slag-heap close to a great perilously-poised "pug" from which, as he now realised, the heat came, and he climbed towards him.

"Ain't 'alf 'ot up 'ere!" said the tramp. "This 'pug's' noo! An' as 'ot as 'ell!"

As he came nearer to it he could hear raindrops sizzling on the "pug" and feel its warmth penetrating his wet clothes. The tramp was lying on the ground, close to the "pug," although its heat was scorching, and Robert could see other forms lying underneath it. If it were to topple over! . . .

"Dig yourself in, mate!" said the tramp. "It's soft 'ere an' warm!"

Robert knelt down and scooped a hole for himself and prepared to lie down in it.

"Tike your coat orf!" the tramp advised, "an' put

it over your 'ead. You'll be all right, then! Warm
as toce!"

"Warm as what?" said Robert.

"Toce! You know! 'Ot buttered toce!"

The tramp lay down and prepared to cover his own
head. "This ain't the best kip I been in," he said,
"but it ain't the worst! You down't get bit by nothink
any'ow—except per'aps a rat or two. I did 'ear once
about a chap that 'ad his fice 'alf ate orf by rats——!"

Robert hurriedly pulled his coat over his head and
mercifully heard no more.

He lay in the warm dust unable to sleep. His plight
was one that he had never imagined himself likely
to be in. Here he was, a Dunwoody, lying on a hill
with tramps and hooligans, soaked to the skin, hungry,
chivvied by the police! His descent to this misery
had been unaccountably swift. He had dropped in a
few hours from a comfortable home and abundant food
and a sufficiency of money to a hole in a slag-heap and
the company of the lowest of the low! . . . He suddenly sat up and listened. It seemed to him that some
one had moved, but although he strained hard to hear
no sound reached him. He had imagined it. Queer
that he should be so nervous. The least thing seemed
to upset him. And he could not sleep! His mind was
crammed full of thoughts, jumping about and tormenting him. He put out his hand to feel if rain were
still falling. Only a few light drops fell on it. Well,
thank goodness, the wet was over. Perhaps in this
warm dust his clothes would dry. If he were to move
nearer to the "pug," the heat would soon dry them!
. . . He stood up and gazed about him. The moon
was struggling to break her way through the thick

clouds that ran so swiftly past her that she could make
no impression on them, but now and then they paused
in their flight and allowed her to look through the
gap in their ranks. In such a moment he saw the whole
of the waste-land spreading before him and softened
and made gentle by the moonlight. Down there, far,
far down, it seemed, lay the green lake, dark and deep.
When the moon's beams shone on it, it seemed to be
kindly, but when the moon was withdrawn behind
clouds and only the red and orange flames from the
iron-foundry shone on it, it seemed terribly evil. The
moon made it look like smooth grass; the foundry-fires
made it look like a great glistening baleful eye! . . .
He turned quickly. Something had cracked. Dis-
tinctly he had heard the sound of cracking. He did
not hear it again, although he listened for what seemed
a long while, and presently he lay down in the warm,
white dust and tried to sleep. His eyes were closed
and his thoughts were quiet—in a few moments he
would be asleep—when again he heard the sound of
cracking, much louder this time than before, and then,
before he could sit up, there was a terrific noise as
if the earth had exploded, and a piece of stone fell on
him and cut one of his hands. He heard a loud scream
and the sound of something falling. . . . He sprang
up from the ground in time to see the "pug" rolling
down the slag-heap to the green pool, and as he looked,
the moon shone for a moment through the clouds, and
he saw that something was rolling with it! . . . The
moon was hidden again and only the red and orange
flames were left for light! He heard a great splash
and saw the green surface of the pool break and turn

black like an enormous mouth opening. Then the mouth slowly closed, and the pool became green again.

V

The sound of the explosion had sent the sleeping men leaping from their beds, and they stood about the place where the "pug" had been, terror-stricken. The rain had ceased, and the moon's long struggle with the clouds had ended in victory for her. The whole of the slag-heap was lit with her pale light, and the frightened men could be plainly seen cowering together, their long shadows stretching down the white dust. Robert could hear a white-faced, terrified man, repeating the same words over and over. "Whit'll I dae! Whit'll I dae!" He could feel his lips trembling as he walked towards the group. "What's happened?" he said to the man nearest to him.

"Says his mate's down there!" was the reply.

"Down there?"

"Aye! He was underneath it when it burst, an' it rolled him down——!"

Robert grabbed hold of the man's arm. "Do you mean to say there's a man drownin' down there?" he cried.

"Droonin'!" another man answered. "Drooned, you mean. If he wisna deed afore he wis drooned. He'll be deep in mud the noo, wi' tons o' 'pug' on top o' him for a tombstone!"

"Can't we do something?" Robert asked.

"Dae somethin'? Whit can we dae? The man's deed, an' buried deep doon there. Whit can we dae?"

"An' not the first yin eether!" said another voice. "Nor the last!" said another.

Robert turned away, feeling sick. He struggled up to the top of the slag-heap and sat down. He could see dark figures standing together and hear the sound of their voices as they argued about the explosion. The tramp who had guided him here was asserting in his shrill Cockney voice that there ought to be "compensytion" for the death of the man who had been drowned. "Somebody ought to p'y damages for this— 'eavy damages!" His voice drifted across the slag-heap, oddly irritating to hear. Him and his compensation! At the foot of the slag-heap, Robert could discern the drowned man's mate, distractedly peering into the pool. Now and then he poked a stick into the green water! . . .

There was a warm "pug" lying near him, and Robert rose and moved closer to it, so that its heat might dry his clothes. The men below him, tired of the Cockney tramp's eloquence, were separating. A few of them lit a fire under a "pug" and crowded round it for the rest of the night, but the majority of them crept back into the holes in which they had been sleeping when the "pug" exploded. Quietness began to settle upon them. A faint murmur that grew fainter and presently ceased came from the men gathered round the red glow of their fire. The drowned man's mate still peered into the pool! . . . The sky lightened and the clouds broke into long strips that slowly changed colour. Behind the black bars of cloud, he could see cold silver and pale lemon light that grew warm and warmer until the black bars of cloud turned orange and then red and, finally, the sun stripped the darkness from the sky and filled the heaven with bright light and made the black sky blue and turned the thick masses of cloud into balls of white smoke. He could hear sleepy birds twittering and then, their eyes wide open, he could hear them boldly singing. He could see the sleeping tramps now quite plainly, lying in their scooped beds. The men who had lit the fire under the "pug," were prone on the ground, asleep. At the foot of the slag-heap, he could see another form, the drowned man's mate, huddled and asleep on the verge of the green pool! . . . And now the world began to awake. Workmen appeared in the distance hurrying to their jobs, and he could see signs of commencing labour in the clay-pits. He put out his hand and touched a tuft of blackened grass striving to grow on the slag. It was wet with dew. Little spangled drops of dew gleamed on the dark grass like shining crystals! . . . He got up and stretched himself, and walked down the slag-heap and returned to the town. He seemed suddenly to himself to be a grown man.

VI

He had already earned two shillings and a meal when he met the sailor, heavy with drink and "dunnage," and the sailor, in a fit of drunken generosity, had given him another shilling for helping him aboard the four-masted barque, *Ardrossan Castle,* lying out in the river. "Whash you wanna be a sailor for?" he muttered, when he heard Robert asking how he, too, might go to sea. "Nobody but a born idjit would go to sea!"

"Well, how do you go anyway?" Robert persisted.

"Ever been before?"

"No."

"Well, don't go now. Thash my advice——!"

"I want to go. There's nothin' else I want to do!"

"Well, go as a pass—pass—— Well, go as a pass-hager, then. Thash only shenshabble way to go to sea! Here, just help me to stow this stuff——!"

They were in the forecastle, an ill-lit, congested place, and the sailor was trying to put his dunnage away and at the same time cope with his "donkey's breakfast," or straw-stuffed mattress. "Fanshy wantin' to be a sailor!" he said more to himself than to Robert. "Whash the marrer with the jails, eh, whash the marrer with 'em that you wanna go she—sea——" He suddenly dropped the mattress and turned to Robert. "Ever heard of Dr. Johnson?" he demanded. Robert shook his head. "Ah! Ah!" the sailor said, wagging his finger wisely. "Very clever man, he was, very clever man. He said nobody should go to she—sea, I mean, that could get into jail! Thash what he said, an' he was qui' ri'! Qui' ri' he was! You take my tip, boy, you go to jail! Far better for you!"

"You're drunk!" said Robert.

"I know that! I know I'm drunk. Why shouldn't I be drunk! I' ave a ri' to be drunk, 'aven't I? . . ."

Robert left him, and returned to the deck. A man was standing at the side of the ship looking down on the Clyde.

"Excuse me, sir!" said Robert.

The man spat into the river and then turned and looked at Robert without speaking.

"Do you want a man!" said Robert.

"Man! What age are you?"

"Twenty-one," Robert boldly replied.

"You're young-looking for your age! Have you ever been on a boat before?"

"No, sir!"

"I shouldn't think so, either! Twenty-one are you?"

"Yes, sir!"

"Will you take your oath on that!"

"I will," said Robert.

The man paused for a few moments, and then said, "Where's your family live!"

"I have no family," Robert replied.

"Well, where did they live when you had one?"

"Belfast, sir! My father was a seafarin' man. He was drowned in the Pacific——!"

"An' you want to be drowned, too, I suppose?"

"He was the master of his ship!" Robert proudly replied.

"Was he? Well, I'm the second mate of this one! Come back in a couple of hours' time an' see the captain!"

"Thank you, sir. Can I stay aboard now!"

"No, you can't! Bring your dunnage with you in case he signs you on. We sail in the mornin'!"

"I haven't any!"

"Have you nothin' but what you've on?"

"No, sir!"

"Oh, well! Your family seems to have left you badly off! You'll need stuff of some sort—sea-boots an' a change of clothes, anyway! You'd better get some!"

"I've no money!"

"My God, boy, you talk as if you'd just arrived in the world! . . . Well, come back in two hours. I'll talk to the captain about you!"

He went ashore, and stood on the quay for a while gazing at the ship on which he hoped to sail. She looked lovely as she sat on the water, with her long, slender lines stretching from her beautiful bow to her heavy stern. "I hope to my God," he said to himself, "I get aboard her!"

Two hours later the mate told him that he could go to the agent's office and sign on as an ordinary seaman. He could draw a month's pay in advance and had better buy himself a pair of sea-boots and overalls. "Get as much as you can," he said, "you'll need it all. This ship's going to Australia! . . ."

THE SECOND PART

OF

THE WAYWARD MAN

Where the remote Bermudas ride
In the ocean's bosom unespied,
From the small boat that row'd along
The listening winds received this song:
   "What should we do but sing His praise
   That led us through the watery maze
   Unto an isle so long unknown
   And yet far kinder than our own?
   Where lie the huge sea-monsters wracks,
   That lift the deep upon their backs,
   He lands us on a grassy stage,
   Safe from the storms' and prelates' rage:
   He gave us this eternal Spring
   Which here enamels everything,
   And sends the fowls to us in care
   On daily visits through the air:
   He hangs in shades the orange bright
   Like golden lamps in a green night,
   And does in the pomegranates close
   Jewels more rich than Ormus shows:
   He makes the figs our mouths to meet
   And throws the melons at our feet;
   But apples plants of such a price,
   No tree could ever bear them twice.
   With cedars chosen by His hand
   From Lebanon He stores the land;
   And makes the hollow seas that roar
   Proclaim the ambergris on shore.
   He cast (of which we rather boast)
   The Gospel's pearl upon our coast,
   And in these rocks for us did frame
   A temple where to sound His name.
   O, let our voice His praise exalt
   Till it arrive at Heaven's vault;
   Which thence (perhaps) rebounding may
   Echo beyond the Mexique bay!"
Thus sung they in the English boat
A holy and a cheerful note:
And all the way, to guide their chime,
With falling oars, they kept the time.

                   ANDREW MARVELL.

THE FIRST CHAPTER

I

THE tug sounded her syren, and soon afterwards the *Ardrossan Castle* moved down the Clyde to begin her trip to Melbourne. She lay well down in the water, for she was heavily loaded with pig-iron, steel rails, cement, pianos, sewing machines and lighter cargo. She straightened herself out in the river as the tug slowly pulled her along, and seemed to Robert, as he stood with the rest of the crew on the forecastle-deck, to be the most beautiful ship in the world. He was trembling with excitement. Now, indeed, was he committed to adventure. He was a seaman aboard a boat bound for Australia. The miseries he had endured on the slag-heap remained in his memory merely as events, disagreeable when they were experienced, but romantic to remember. Already he had created an impression by narrating his story to Wadsworth, the sailor, now sober, in whose company he had come aboard the *Ardrossan Castle,* and Wadsworth had insisted that the story should be repeated to the rest of the crew. The story would entertain others; he must not forget any of it! . . . People on shore were shouting and cheering as the ship moved down to wider and deeper water, and Robert, cheering back to them with his comrades, felt as if they were his friends who had come to see him off on his first long voyage. The

165

dripping clouds of yesterday had vanished and in their place was a high blue heaven that turned the river and the sea almost to the colour of turquoise. The wind was cold, but pleasant, and it sent the water splashing against the ship's sides with a sound like the cracking of a whip. He leant over the lee rail and watched the water dividing at the bow, rising up in clear, shining arches with silvery-white crests, as the ship was drawn down the river. This was an easy time for the crew, but presently, when the tug had cast off and the yards had to be manned and the sails spread! . . . He glanced up at the tall varnished masts and beautifully-spread yards and felt his heart, for a moment, sink as he thought of himself perched high among them in a gale, striving with broken, bleeding fingers, to set sail! . . . But his fear quickly passed. If other men could do it, he also could do it. All of them on board that boat had had to go aloft for the first time once in their lives, and no doubt their hearts sank then as his sank now, and when he looked at some of them, he thought that he could easily do what such poor-looking men had done! . . . Anyhow, whatever he was told to do, he would do. It was unlikely that he would be asked to do anything that could not be done, and if anybody else could do it, he could do it!

The ship came to for a little time at the Tail of the Bank, while the jib-boom was rigged out and some final stores were brought on board, and then she sailed into the Gareloch to have her compasses adjusted. The wind had risen and the clouds had darkened, and the captain, scanning the sky, ordered the tug to tow him into Lamlash Bay where they lay under the Arran hills for the night; but on the next day, although the gale had not abated, they spread their sails and beat out to the open sea.

"The old man's goin' to chance it!" said Wadsworth to Robert. "An' this is where you'll get it in the neck if you ain't a born sailor. Sick that's what you'll be! Sick as a dog!"

II

But he had not been ill. Marvellously he had found his sea-legs. The ship plunged and rolled in the swirling water, dipping and rising so that she seemed, now to be high above the sea and now about to be submerged in it, and at first, as she rolled over on her side as if she would never recover her balance, he felt that he was about to be sick. But the sensation passed. "I'm a born sailor!" he said to himself. "This is my da in me!" A sweet pride filled him at the thought. He had taken to the sea as if it were his by right. He was a sailor. The novelty of seafaring was strong in him. Everything on the ship interested him. The "old man," Captain Craig, aloof on the poop-deck and famous among the famous captains of clippers, filled him with awe. That small, stern-looking, bearded man could control the sea and the wind and the sky; he could take a ship across deep and wide waters and bring her back again with no more agitation than Alec would display in selling a gallon of paraffin oil; he knew about tides and stars and gales and could cause the sun to tell him just where he was on an empty ocean. Talk about ministers and high-up people like Mr.—Mr.—what was the name of that man his mother was related to! . . . De Lacy, that was the name—

talk about people like that being anybody when there was a man like Captain Craig in the world! Ridiculous! The mates, the crew, the rigging, the masts— wherever he looked, whatever he saw, seemed to be incessantly enthralling. He had watched the crew settling into the ship, lugging out their chests and showing off their shore-going vanities; and had helped a hard-bitten old shellback to decorate the forecastle with pictures torn from magazines. The central place was given to a coloured print of a dancing-girl whose long legs and full thighs were clad in pink tights that might have been her skin. There was a sort of belt round her waist, pink, too, and with a golden fringe on it, and over her breasts were things that looked like shallow bowls! . . . Robert felt ashamed, yet daring, as he held the picture while Masters prepared to tack it to the riding-bitts.

"That must be a desperate woman!" he said, when the picture was tacked up.

"Desperate! What do you mean, desperate!" Masters said.

"Showing her legs like that, I should think she was a bad woman!"

"Bad my granny!" Masters said. "What harm's in showin' a good pair of legs to the world? When you've been in this damned ship for four months without sight or sign of a woman, you'll be grateful for a peep at her!" He tapped the picture with his knuckles as he spoke. "I've been a sailor all my life, an' I tell you this, a man gets hungry for the sight of a woman —just to see an' look at one—when he's been on the water for months an' seen nothin' but men! I always take a picture like that with me whatever ship I go

on. It's a great comfort to a man, a picture like
that!"

Robert wondered. He had never thought of women
as necessary to men, so necessary that merely to look
at one was comforting. His mother, of course—but
she was different. Brenda Cairnduff, now, he could
scarcely imagine himself "thinking long" about her,
though Brenda was a nice-looking girl. She would
probably marry Alec. One of these days, a long time
hence, he would go home and there he would see
Brenda, married to Alec, and the mother of two or
three children! . . . He would be their uncle! . . .
The reflection diverted his mind to other thoughts,
and suddenly he was full of apprehension. When
would he return to his home? This voyage to Melbourne would take several months; the journey back
would take several more; the ship might not immediately return to Glasgow; he might not see home again
for years, and in that time his mother might die! . . .
The joy that had filled his heart as he felt his feet
gripping the deck like a born sailor's feet now fled
from it, and when Masters had done decorating the
forecastle, Robert crept into his bunk and turned his
face to the ship's side. He could hear the murmur
of talk from the other men, continual praise of the
"last ship I was in" and gloomy prophecies concerning
the discomforts and miseries likely to be endured in
the *Ardrossan Castle,* and he could see through the
porthole the stars rising and falling within its circle as
the ship moved through the sea. But it was not of his
comrades' talk nor was it of the stars that he was thinking. His mind was full of pictures of his home and
one persistent, terrible thought, that he might never

see his mother again. He realised the anxiety she must feel about him, and the thought that she would lie awake at night, wondering where he was, daunted him. He might have sent a postcard to her to tell her that he was safe and sound, but he had not sent one, and now it was too late. He seemed to himself to be cruel, wantonly inflicting pain on her! . . . He would write to her from Melbourne and tell her not to worry about him. But if he were to do that she might have him fetched back to Belfast. He had sworn a lie about his age! . . . He heard five bells struck, and knew that his watch below would soon be ended. He must try to sleep, and so resolving he closed his eyes. But presently, almost without his knowledge, they were open again, and again he was staring at the stars through the porthole. It was useless to try to sleep, so he sat up in his bunk and looked out of the port-hole. The sky was full of stars, millions of them. They seemed to him like seeds sown on a big, dark ploughed field. He imagined God striding across the sky, throwing fistfuls of star-dust about the heavens as a sower throws fistfuls of corn. Presently the seed would sprout and the stars would grow and the big dark field of heaven would flourish with flowers and grain and grass! . . . He listened to the cold, swishing noise of the sea, and felt now and then spray flicking his face. The sea never stopped moving. There was no rest on the sea. The tide came in and went out and came in again and went out again. The stars seemed to be still, but he had read somewhere that they too continually moved. Everything in the world moved. But where was everything moving to? Sadness filled him. The sea and the stars and this ship were beautiful

yet they made him feel sorrowful! . . . He heard footsteps descending into the forecastle, and he turned his
head and saw the man on the anchor-watch come in
and light his pipe. He looked at Robert, and then
came and stood by his bunk for a moment.

"Homesick, sonny?" he said.

"Yes," Robert replied.

"Everybody is," he said, "at sea! Better get some
sleep if you can. It'll be eight bells soon!"

He went out, and Robert laid himself down again
in his bunk. The forecastle was dark, except where
red slits of light gleamed through chinks in the stove.
He could hear the deep breathing of his sleeping comrades and the incessant beat of the sea, and as he
listened his eyes filled with tears. Presently eight bells
was struck, and his watch below was ended. He pulled
on his boots and went on deck.

III

The second mate had chosen him for the starboard-
watch. Including the second and third mates, there
were twelve men in the watch, one of whom, Charlie
Stephens, became Robert's watch-mate, looking after
the binnacles at the beginning of the trip and keeping
the time at night in their watch. Stephens was an
Etonian—there came a time when Robert felt that of
all the boys who had run away from home, he alone
had not been educated at Eton—and had led the sort
of adventurous life that Robert wished to lead. He
had sailed all over the seven seas and said that he knew
China better than he knew Windsor. There was very
little that any one could tell him about 'Frisco. He

knew a few "joints" in New York, and if his name were mentioned to certain people in Honolulu it would make a profound impression upon them. He had served in an American regiment, but, failing to like it, had deserted and taken to the sea again. What puzzled him, he frequently said, was how he contrived to get to Glasgow. If any one had asked him which was the last place on earth that he, Stephens, was likely to visit, he would have replied, "Glasgow." Yet to Glasgow he had come. Moreover he had been ill in Glasgow. A fever had seized him there, and he was taken to hospital. He had nothing against Glasgow. It seemed to him to be a pretty decent sort of city, but he could not understand how he had managed to get into it! . . . Stephens was a good seaman, plucky, stout-hearted, astonishingly cheerful, and he talked in a comic way that extraordinarily amused Robert, who had started by believing all that Stephens told him, but soon learned to disbelieve most of it. "No," said Stephens, "I don't tell lies; I tell stories!"

"You *are* a liar, Charlie!" Robert insisted.

"I'm a romancer!"

But whatever he was, Stephens was a good comrade and it was he, more than any person, who made a seaman of Robert. He saw that Robert knew nothing at all of ships, and he had set himself to teach him seamanship. They climbed the forecastle-head and began on the flying-jib downhaul, and worked their way aft to the spanker-boom sheet, Stephens naming ropes and gear and explaining their uses, while Robert strove hard to remember them. "Do you see this string?" he said, shaking it so that Robert could see it moving for the whole of its length. "See where it goes to?

Right up to that block on the fore royal stay! See?"
He shook the buntline again.

"Yes," said Robert, and then, "What's it called?"
"The fore royal buntline!"

At first, the running gear seemed to Robert to be an
untidy mess, and he wondered how any sailor could
ever disentangle the ravel of ropes which ran from the
rails to the mastheads and yards, but very soon he
realised that this tangle was no tangle, but a most
severe order. Every rope had a name and a place and
a purpose, and no rope must be put out of its place.
The safety of the ship depended upon the certainty
that a sailor could go to a belaying-pin and find there
the rope that should be on it. "A hell of a mess we'd
be in if a chap had to go hunting in the dark in a gale
for a rope that was one day here and another day over
there. So get that fact into your noddle first. Every
rope has one place and no other place! Got that!"

"Yes, Charlie!"

"Do you twig anything odd about these ropes?"

Robert thought that everything about them was odd.

"Yes, but do you notice anything in particular about
them!"

"No."

"Well, notice this!" He took hold of a rope as he
spoke and shook it. "See how high it goes?"

"Yes," Robert replied, following the rope with his
eye up to the fore lower rigging.

"And how far aft it runs!" Robert nodded his head.
"That's another fact to get into your noddle. The
higher a rope leads aloft, the further aft it leads on
deck, and the lower down it leads, the further forward.
Is that sticking in your skull?"

"It's stuck," said Robert.

In this way, they went more than once through the whole running gear of the ship because, though Robert strove hard to remember all the names, he could not at once do so.

"And if you're going to be any good at this job," Stephens said, "don't hang back when an order's given! Jump to it! It's a sailor's deepest disgrace to be called by name to do a job. Jump to it! And the nastier it is, the quicker you should jump! Do you want to be a sailor, Darkie, or a rope-hauler!"

Here, too, he was called Darkie.

"A sailor," he said.

"Well, never let yourself be named for a job. You wait till we get a smell of the Cape, and you'll soon see who are the sailors on this ship and who are the rope-haulers. That fellow, Jennings, is a bit of a rope-hauler! He can do the job all right if he likes, but he's too darned lazy to try. You watch him in the next rough weather. You won't find him first in the rigging or laying out on the yard-arm; he'll be in the forecastle hunting for his oilskins, if he can sneak away, and he'll hug the bunt, if he can't, as if it were his girl!"

Robert swore to himself that he would always be found as far out on the yard-arm as he could get. No bunt-hugging for him! . . .

It was Charlie who had told him about the stars so that he could identify them. At school, they had been spots in a picture of chalk-marks on a blackboard totally unrelated to the lovely lights that hung from the sky, and so little had his instruction in astronomy interested him that he began to believe that all knowledge of the stars must be dull. What did their names matter anyhow? Who cared how far or how near they

were to the earth? It was enough for him that the
heavens were full of stars and that, on a clear frosty
night, he could see them split on the sky like primroses
in a hedge. If primroses were to be lit up at night,
gleaming and glowing in the grass, the hedgerows and
meadows would resemble the floor of heaven! . . .
Mr. Mineely talked about stars as if he had never seen
one. He drew diagrams and said "That's Venus!" or
"That's Mars!" and then rubbed the diagram out with
a chalky duster. The Milky Way was a thing you
drew on a blackboard and then wiped out! . . . Mr.
Mineely knew exactly how many miles separated the
planet—a word Robert loathed—Venus from the Sun
and knew all about its diameter, but once when Robert,
walking home with him in the evening, asked him to
say which of the stars they saw clustered above their
heads was Venus, he hesitated and hummed and ha'ad
and finally said, pointing to one, that he thought that
that must be it. Robert had had to be content with
that information; for nobody that he knew then could
tell him any more. But Charlie Stephens not only
knew the names of the stars, but could identify them
and make them tell him where he was on the sea. He
did not know the order of the planets in importance
nor how far they were from the sun nor could he even
estimate their diameter, but he knew and recognised
them and told Robert how to recognise them, too, and
in quiet spells in night-watches, Robert and he would
stand on the forecastle-head and gaze at the stars casting their trembling reflections on the dark sea. Up,
there, astern, and in line with the mizzen-truck were
the Pointers and west from them and half-way up the
horizon was the North Star—the sailors' friend. The
whole constellation of heaven seemed to be laid bare

before him, though Charlie's knowledge was elementary, and Robert, for the first time in his life, felt that earth and sea and sky and stars and men were bound together. The Great Bear and the Little Bear and the Pleiades and the Heavenly Twins, the Hyades with Aldebaran, the Bull's Eye, fiercely shining in the middle of them, and Orion and Mars and Sirius, the Dog Star, the brightest in heaven, and the Great Nebula, stardust carelessly spilt, as if God the sower had suddenly emptied His sackful of stars and the wind had scattered them across the sky. Mr. Mineely's lessons in astronomy now seemed very ridiculous and insufficient to Robert. He stood in silence by Stephen's side, murmuring in his mind the names he had heard recited to him, and was content. Spray flicked his face, and he could taste salt in the wind. The deck heaved slowly under his feet as if the ship were mounting to the stars. How lovely was the world! . . . He heard the second mate, who was pacing the poop-deck, calling to him to take a trick at the wheel, and he went aft and took hold of the spokes and repeated the course. He could feel the rudder kicking, and a queer joy filled his heart, as he put the helm down and watched the main royal slowly lift and fill. The ship had answered and was obedient to him. He was driving her through the sea. A little while ago he was a boy at school, bidden by his mother, but now he was a seaman, taking a turn at the wheel, and making a ship obey him. He raised his eyes to the stars again. There they were, all of them, Aldebaran and Sirius, the Gemini and Orion, star-dust and the Pleiades and the one sure star in heaven, the North Star that would guide a sailor anywhere above the Equator and bring him safely home! . . . He repeated the course to himself again. "Full and by!"

And again he pressed the helm down and saw once more the clew of the main royal lift and fill, and felt the ship move to obey him.   And his heart thrilled. He was a sailor.

IV

The Bay of Biscay disappointed Robert.   In all the sea-books he had read, the authors insisted on the terrors of that stormy sea.   Men who had rounded the Horn many times almost without a tremor were seized with frightful misgiving in the Bay.   It was no disgrace to a seaman to be sick in the Bay of Biscay. Captains were queasy on the poop when their ships rolled through that water, and mates became human beings, subject to human weaknesses.   While the *Ardrossan Castle* was still in the Irish Sea, a remark made by Robert revealed his apprehension about the Bay, and immediately his mates filled him with terrible tales of its terrors.   Walls of water rose up and fell upon you.   Sea-gulls became sick when they flew across the Bay.   There was no sailor in the world who did not dread it! . . . Robert remembered the song he had been taught in school:—

> At last the wished-for morrow
>   Broke through the hazy sky,
> Absorbed in silent sorrow
>   Each heaved a bitter sigh.
> The dismal wreck to view
> Struck horror to the crew
>   As she lay on that day
>   In the Bay of Biscay O!

To be wrecked and to toil through the sea in a small boat with little drinking water and no food would be an experience worth having, but merely to be ill in the Bay of Biscay! . . . But the Bay had been as flat as a pancake. "I've seen rougher water on the pond in the Ormeau Park!" Robert scornfully exclaimed to Stephens as he gazed at the still sea. "You're lucky, my lad!" Stephens answered. "But one of these days it'll give you a hell of a doing for catching it in this state! Don't you be so cocky! When you've seen a storm in the Bay you'll respect it!"

He began to believe that the perils of the sea were greatly exaggerated. Fair winds and fine weather had followed them so far almost for the whole of their voyage. Their worst weather had been in the Firth of Clyde. One of the men, a "ranik" like himself, but, unlike him, not a born sailor, had been ill off Ailsa Craig, but had sailed through the Bay without a qualm! That seemed to Robert to be a sore disgrace to the Bay. "If the Clyde could upset him," he said to Stephens, "the Bay should 'a' torn the inside out of him!"

"It'll do that all right in its own time," Stephens replied.

It was their watch below, and they went down together to join their mates, some of whom were playing cards, while others were busy with their dunnage or smoking or asleep. Stephens lay down in his bunk while Robert sat on the end of it, and watched the card-players playing casino. Suddenly he turned to Stephens.

"What made you do this?" he said.

"Do what?"

"Come to sea like this?"

Stephens rolled over on his side. "What made *you* do it?" he answered.

"I ran away!" Robert replied.

Stephens nodded his head. "So did I!"

"But that school you went to—that place called Eton——!"

"Nothing to do with it! This is my life and no other sort would suit me! I'm a misfit!"

"What do you mean, a misfit?"

"Born odd! My father was a bishop, and he had an idea that I ought to grow up and be a bishop too. So he sent me to Eton so that I should get a good start in the profession of St. Peter! Then I was to go to Oxford and on to Ely——!"

"Ely——!"

"Yes! Theological college where only better-class clergy go to be trained! There was a nice refined curacy waiting for me in a select parish behind the Brompton Road in London, and I was to get a minor canonry in a cathedral in the west of England just as soon as father could manage it! Oh, I tell you, it was all nicely arranged. My career was to be very successful! You see, Queen Victoria had a great liking for father!"

"Did you know Queen Victoria?" Robert asked.

"Yes, she patted me on the head once, and gave me a prayer-book when I was confirmed. I was disappointed, for I thought she was going to give me five bob. She was an odd little woman, with big blue eyes that stuck out."

Robert was thrilled. Hitherto the Queen had been almost a myth to him, and he could scarcely believe that he was talking to some one whose head had been patted by her.

"What I can't understand," he said, "is why you

are here. You might have gone into the navy and become an admiral."

"I told you," said Stephens, "this is the only sort of life I'm fit for! I've dog-danced about the world for twenty years, wondering why the devil I was doing it, but I've not yet found out! I suppose I hate the sea as much as any sailor hates it——!"

"Hate the sea!" said Robert in astonishment.

"Loathe the damned thing! All seamen do. But that doesn't keep me off it. There's always a ship somewhere waiting for me to sign on. I can't fit in to that life at home. I'd begin to bite and kick if I had to live like that. I tried it once!"

"What did you do?"

"Went into an office in the City of London! My God, I thought I'd go mad! I sat on a stool at a desk and I wrote things in a book until one day I could stand it no longer and I chucked my pen down on the desk and cleared out. I nearly ran all the way to St. Katherine's Docks where I found a ship! . . . And that finished me with that sort of a life!"

"Didn't your father fret after you?"

"He did. I think he died of grief. I brought his gray hairs in sorrow to the grave——!"

"You're makin' fun of me, Charlie!" Robert protested.

"No, I'm not. He never recovered from the blow to his pride. What was the use of him trotting round the cathedral in full canonicals, when his only son was a common seaman, stinking of tar——!"

Robert was shocked. "That's not the way to talk of your father!" he said.

"Isn't it, Darkie?" Stephens replied, smiling at him,

"You didn't know my father! Anyway, I didn't fit in with the sort of life he wanted me to lead, and that's the sad story of my blighted career. The reason I'm here is because there's no other place for me. I'm a misfit!"

Robert leant back and thought for a few moments. "I wonder if I am, too!" he said at last.

"Probably," Stephen said. "And now, young fellow, clear off my bed. I'm going to sleep!"

He rolled over on his side so that Robert could not see his face and presently he was gently snoring. Robert left his bunk and joined the card-players, who had just finished a game. "Was Charlie tellin' you the story of his life?" one called Scotty said to him. Robert nodded his head. "Did he tell you his father was a bishop?"

"Aye, he did!"

"Well, that's true! It's the only bit about himself he'll ever tell you that is true!"

"He says he's a misfit!" Robert continued.

"Wot the 'ell's that?" demanded Ching the Cockney, who was called by that name because he was reputed to be the grandson of a Chinaman.

"What we all are," Scotty answered. "No bloody good to nobody!"

They were tired of card-playing, and they sprawled about the forecastle while Ching the Cockney and Scotty argued.

"That's abaht it," Ching said. "This 'ere bloody seafarin' life's no cop for a poor bloody sailor—'alf-stahved, 'alf-drahned and not 'alf-pyd. When I wos 'ome last trip, my brother-in-law wot keeps a nam-an'-beef shop in Stoke Nooin'ton took me to a smokin'-

concert, an' so 'elp me Gawd, a chap there sung a song about a life on the ocean wyve, a nome on the rollin' deep——"

"I've heard it!" Scotty said.

"I didden know w'ether to laugh or 'it 'im," Ching continued. " 'E was a clerk in a corn-chandler's shop, 'e was, a little feller with fallen-in eyes an' a waxed moustache, that looked as if a row in the Serpentine 'ud mike 'im sick, an' there 'e was chortlin' 'ard abaht a life on the ocean wyve an' a nome on the rolling deep. I 'ad to laugh! Yus, I thought to meself, you'd be singin' a dam' fine toon if you was lyin' aht on a yard-arm in a bleedin' gyle, tryin' to stretch a syle, an' all you'd 'ad for dinner was pea-soup an' fat pork!"

"Or burgoo mebbe!" said Scotty.

"An' your bleedin' clothes wet through, an' you 'alf dead for a sleep! Ow, yus, a life on the ocean wyve an' a nome on the rollin' deep, I don't think! Wot the 'ell are we all 'ere for?"

A book flew past Ching's head, and Charlie's voice was heard complaining. "How can anybody sleep with you tub-thumping all over the place? If you're so fond of the land, why didn't you stay on it?"

"Well, wot the 'ell *are* we 'ere for?" Ching persisted. "Awnswer me that, somebody!" He paused for a few moments, but no one answered. Then he leant back and said, "Naow, an' I can't awnswer neither! We're 'ere because we can't 'elp our damned selves!"

"Misfits was the word I used!" Charlie exclaimed.

"I dessay! You've always got something comic to say abaht everythink! Any'ow, 'ere we are, an 'ere we'll be 'til we're washed overboard or die of yellow-jack in some God-forsaken 'ole 'undreds of miles from 'ome. If we ain't in this coffin we'll be in another." His mind suddenly diverted from the general misery of a sailor's life to a particular misery. "An' if anybody knows a ship with worse grub than this one, I'd like to 'ear abaht it! Gawd, wot grub!"

Instantly the air was full of foul speech about food; but it all ended in Ching's blasphemous demand to be told where in the world there was a burgoo-jammer to equal the *Ardrossan Castle*. Could any one present tell him of a ship where the pea-soup was waterier and the pork greasier and the burgoo more uneatable than it was on the *Ardrossan Castle*?

"Yes," Charlie interrupted, "I can!"

"Ow, can you! An' wot ship might that be?" Ching said.

"The last ship you were on! And the one before that, and every damned ship you've ever sailed!"

There was laughter then, and the talk became a series of admissions that the food on the ship on which one was serving was always the worst in the world. Robert listened to this talk with a strange sense of depression. Would he, too, come to think of life on the sea as a misery from which there was no escape except by a dismal death?

V

They ran through the north-east trades into the doldrums without incident of any interest, and Robert, now familiar with the ways of the ship, felt that his shipmates complained of the sea with little cause. He felt no boredom or anger when the winds died down or

were so light that the ship seemed to stand still, nor
did he grumble at the sudden squalls of rain and the
thunderstorms.   The men seemed incessantly to be
bracing the yards and the "old man" to be incessantly
manœuvring for movement of some sort, but to Robert
all this trickery with the winds was fascinating.   There
was no need to call him by name; he was eager to run
up the rigging and lie along the yards.   The more he
learned of sail-setting in these calms and light winds,
the better he would be able to work when the gales
blew and the sea rose up and beat the ship about.   His
fear was that he might funk the rigging in a storm and
be content to hug the bunt.   He could imagine with
what scorn Stephens would look at him if he did that.
"Call yourself a sailor!" he would say.   "Why, you're
only a dam' rope-hauler!"   Life was less agreeable in
the doldrums than it had been in the trades.   The ship
would lie, hot and stewing, on unrippled water, and
then, in a trice, dark clouds would leap out of the far
horizon and descend upon her, while lightning flourished across the sky, like a dog shepherding sheep, and
loud thunderclaps rattled round their ears.   The order
would come to take in the light sails and stand by,
and, when all was ready to encounter the storm, it
would veer away from them and again the ship would
lie in a calm sea, with her sails flapping as ineffectively
as a hen's wings.

Sometimes, at night, when the deep dark sky was
lovely with stars, the ship would lie almost still on the
sea that was as deep and dark as the sky, and as lovely
with reflected stars.   She would hang between heaven
and the sea, her spread sails splashed with moonlight

and her yards faintly creaking in the light, listless wind, proud and beautiful. Robert would climb out as far as he could on her brightly-polished jib-boom and gaze on her as a lover gazes on his girl. Her foresails were white with moonshine and so were her main and mizzen topsails, but the rest were dark as velvet, except in little patches where the moonlight pierced between the yards. Here and there a lamp glowed with a red or yellow gleam, and when he looked down on the sea he saw a red or yellow reflection in the trembling water. In these still and silent times he learned to love his ship and realised how sensitive she was, how quickly she answered to the movements of the wind and the sea and threw her masts to the stars as if they were her arms and she would embrace the sky! . . . But the weeks spent in the doldrums were not all spent in such raptures as those. The long hot days were followed by long hot nights, and the watches were full of tedious labour that was often wasted. Hauling and bracing, hauling and bracing to catch any wind that blew, while the sun melted the fat off their bones. The glare of the sun on the sea was intense, and frequently the water would catch a flash of sunlight and reflect it so that one's eyes were dazzled and momentarily blinded. The sea and the ship began to smell of the sun, a long, hot, sweaty smell that seemed stifling! . . . The *Ardrossan Castle* seemed suddenly to be very small. There was no room in which to get away from other people, no place in which a man could be alone. Solitude, for which he had felt no desire before, now became a necessity. His shipmates were too familiar to him, and he felt in himself a disgust with them, even with Charlie

Stephens. They were always there. He tired of their talk. Ching the Cockney was the Philadelphia lawyer of the crew, and his flat, ugly voice continually repeated a tale of injustice! . . . Robert had never realised how boring a word could become until he had heard Ching say "bleedin' " for what appeared to be the millionth time. He would lie out on a yard to brace a flapping sail and hear Ching cursing the "bleedin' 'eat" and "this bleedin' burgoo-jammer" and the "bleedin' sea" and "this bleedin' life!" . . . He would descend to the deck and again he would hear Ching adjuring some "bleedin' " thing or other. In the forecastle, while he tossed on his heat-swollen bunk, he still heard Ching cursing. . . . It was useless for him to try to sleep while this inane clatter went on, and he turned on his side to listen. Ching was in full cry. "Women!" he said, and then laughed derisively. "Wot I don't know abaht women ain't 'ardly worth knowin'!"

"Fat lot you know, Ching——!"

"Ow! An' wot the bleedin' 'ell do you know abaht wot I know?" Ching snarled back.

Robert turned away again. This sort of talk would continue until the end of the dog-watch.

"I've 'ad women all over the bleedin' globe. White women an' black women an' brown women an' yellow women, an' I'll tell you somethink. W'en you've 'ad one woman, you've 'ad all the women! I know wot I'm bleedin' well talkin' about!"

Robert sat up in his bunk. "Can't you think of anything else to say but 'bleedin'!" he shouted.

Ching looked at him as if he could not believe his ears. "Was you talkin' to me?" he said.

"Aye, I was," Robert boldly replied. "I'm sick, sore

an' tired of hearin' you call everythin' bleedin'! For Jases' sake, think of another word!"

Ching strode over to Robert's bunk. "Ow, you're sick, sore *an'* tired, are you, of 'earin' me say 'Bleedin'! Are you? Well, we'll 'ave to 'ave a little practice in syin' it, so that we can get used to it. Nah, then, my bantam, sit up an' sy 'Bleedin'! 'til I tell you to stop!"

He seized Robert by the collar of his shirt and dragged him from his bunk. "Nah," he said, "after me——!"

Robert tried to twist out of Ching's grip, but could not do so. "Let me go!" he shouted.

"Ow, naow, not 'til you've done your recitation, little Willie. Ow, kimmon, nah——!"

Robert kicked out and caught Ching on the shin, and Ching, howling with pain, let him go.

"You'll mebbe leave me alone after that," said Robert. Ching did not answer. He rushed at Robert, lunging at him as he ran, and caught him a horrible blow in the face that sent him reeling against one of the uprights.

"I'll leave you alone," he said, "when I've knocked 'ell aht of you. Git up! Git up, you barstard!" He hauled Robert to his feet and then knocked him down again. There was a movement among the other men in the forecastle. "That's enough of that, Ching!" one of them said. "'E's 'ad 'is doin'!"

"Naow, 'e ain't then. Not 'alf 'ad it! An' I down't want no lip from none of you, neither. I'm cock of this walk, I am, see!" He turned again to Robert. "Git up!" he bawled at him. Robert did not move, and Ching kicked him in the ribs. As he did so, Charlie Stephens came down the stairs. "God," he said, "but

it's hot!" Then he saw Robert lying on the floor and
Ching kicking him. He did not speak. He seemed to
leap from the ladder to Ching's side. He seized him
by the scruff of his neck and turned him round.

"Get your shirt off!" Stephens said.

"What you mean——?"

"Get your damned shirt off or I'll tear it off!"

"Oo's interferin' with you, eih! I was 'ittin' 'im,
not you!"

"I know you were, and now I'm going to hit you for
a change. I'm about your match, and he's not. Are
you goin' to take your shirt off or shall I take it off
for you!"

"I don't want to fight you," Ching snivelled.

"But I want to fight you, Ching. I just want to
smash your face for you. I've a feeling that your nose
would look better if it was round at the back of your
neck! . . . Take your shirt off, damn you, or I'll
strangle you with it!"

All the fight was out of Ching now, but he slowly
stripped, and then, with a yell, rushed at Stephens,
whirling his fists wildly. He was instantly sent floundering back again by a blow on the chin that made his
teeth rattle. He stood for a moment gulping and
dazed and then rushed on Stephens again. He dropped
on to the floor, thrown there by a frightful punch in
the face that made him feel as if his eyes had been
squelched out of their sockets.

"Any time you want a thick ear," said Charlie, "you
just let me know, and I'll give it to you!" He sat down
beside Robert. "That's the only thing I ever learnt at
Eton," he said.

"What?" Robert replied.

"How to hit a chap a punch on the jaw. I must show you how to do it!"

"Right you are," said Robert.

VI

The south-east trades came upon them in a rage, and they passed, almost instantly, from intense heat and thin winds into cold air and heavy winds. There was no end to their work. They had overhauled the rigging and set up new braces and patched and repaired the heavy sails and made themselves ready for the storms that were coming to them; and scarcely had they done so than the barometer bumped. The wind rose and howled at them, and the sky filled with hurrying masses of dead gray clouds, and the sea grew angrier and rougher. There were no sea-gulls now flying in their wake, but only shrill, shrieking Cape pigeons and a single albatross that flew into the wind with scarcely any movement of its big, beautiful wings. The great bird seemed not to feel the wind beating against its breast. It could not rest on the rough water, but it lay at ease on the rough wind. There was no time for idling now, or lounging through a watch. Sail had to be shortened and the boats specially lashed and the ship put in shape for the storm whose rage rose steadily from a heavy wind to a strong gale. They stripped down to the fore and main lower topsails and reefed foresail as the gale grew fiercer, and in the morning found great seas flopping over their weather rail, each wave seeming to be bigger than the rest. Robert saw the seas rising up and flinging themselves on the ship and was amazed when he found her still afloat. It

seemed impossible that she should not drown in the
great mountains of water that fell upon her, and when
the gale became a hurricane and drove the sea with
such violence against the bulwarks that the planking
was torn from the stanchions and washed away, he felt
certain that presently the ship would sink. The daylight dripped away and was followed by a black night.
All hands were now wearing the ship in the hope that
better weather might be made on the other tack, and,
creeping under her battered bulwarks lest they should
be washed overboard, they stretched life-lines along the
deck on to which great waves continually fell.

"All right, sonny?" Charlie yelled to Robert as they
manned the braces. The water was up to their waists
as he yelled.

"Yes, Charlie!" Robert answered, though he imagined himself almost a drowned man.

He glanced up at the dark, staggering masts, and felt
fear when he thought of himself out on the yards,
struggling to fold a sail against the wind that blew
it almost out of his control. His imagination stole his
courage from him; he could see himself, with torn and
bleeding fingers striving to push the canvas back, and
then, through standing on a rotten rope or because the
wind was too strong for him, losing his hold and falling
into the black cauldron! . . . For a moment he hung
back. After all, this was his first trip and his first
storm. There were others who knew the job better
than he did! . . . He caught sight of Ching cowering
in the dark, and the sight stiffened him. "By God,"
he said to himself, "he's a bunt-hugger——!" And he
followed Charlie, though his heart was in his mouth
as he felt the ship lurch and reel and knew that a slip

would throw him into the sea and that he could not hope to be saved from it.

The ship wore round to the port tack, slipping slowly between the heavy seas, but the change was useless, and presently a great pile of water crashed on to them, smashing a boat and carrying away the galley smoke-stack. The water poured down the pipe-hole, putting out the fire and flooding the galley. "That finishes our coffee," Charlie shouted in Robert's ear.

More seas poured upon them ripping and tearing their way aft, until the whole ship was wet and wounded and sore from the pounding that the seas gave her sides. The old man decided to run before the storm, and once more the tired seamen were busy with their gear. They clewed up the foresail and took in the top-sails, and then, clinging to the life-lines, manned the braces again until the ship was headed before the wind. When she was round, she suddenly leapt forward as if she had been struck, and raced along, plunging and rearing, while sea after sea rolled over her sides, two seas meeting mid-way on the deck with a loud cracking noise and hurling great spires of green spray into the air which whipped it white and scattered it along the ship's length. When Robert, for a moment, looked forward, he saw the black masts reeling in pools of boiling white suds, and creaking as if their fibres were being torn apart. A horrible feeling of impotence and solitude possessed him. He and his comrades were helpless. All this rope-hauling and sail-clewing and wearing and tacking was useless; the sea was too strong for them; a single wave could swing over the side and annul all their efforts to save themselves and their ship. The thought that presently he would drown appalled him when he reflected that no one at home would ever know what had become of him. He was not afraid of drowning, although he deeply desired to live, but unaccountably he felt himself afraid of an unfriended burial! . . . But these melancholy thoughts did not long continue to fill his mind. Orders were yelled against the wind and presently the ship, with most of her sails reefed and the rest flapping in the wind, was sufficiently settled for one watch to go below and shed their clothes and get some sleep. Robert's watch climbed on to the main rail so that they might get out of the way of the water that washed across the deck, and there, clinging how they could, they stayed, wet to the skin, while the sea grew stronger and more violent and the great waves hammered the ship's stern, making her shudder as if she were about to split. The sky was as black as tar. No moon nor any stars lit the heavens, but there was a ghastly white phosphorescent glow over the sea as if the moon had died and its ghost were haunting the waves. Robert looked up at Charlie who had climbed beside him.

"It's a bit rough," he said.

"Rough!" Charlie replied. "This isn't rough! Wait 'til you get a real stinker of a storm!"

"D'you get worse than this, then?"

"Darkie, my boy, you'll not be a sailor 'til you soak your corns in salt water going round the Horn! This is only a taster——!"

"God!" said Robert to himself.

Suddenly the main topsail broke with a terrific noise, and the iron chain sheet was flung about in the wind as if it were whip-cord. When it struck the yard-arm sparks flew into the air and in a little while it had

ripped the sail from top to bottom. All hands were
ordered up to stow the broken sail, and then the ship,
like a bird with a torn wing thrashed, but more slowly
now, before the storm. Her diminished speed made her
easier for the sea to board, and great masses of green
water flecked with white foam climbed over the stern
and leaped across the after-house on to the deck below,
where they fell on the men who were lashed to the
wheel and for a while submerged them. Then when
it seemed to Robert that the sea was beginning to
subside, he saw coming over the stern an enormous
wall of water. He heard a yell of warning and leaped
at the boom and flung his arms tightly around it, and
as he did so, the sea fell on him and tried to tear his
arms away from the spanker. He was drowning. Tons
of water were falling on his head. The weight of them
would sink the ship. He could hear a tremendous
roaring noise and he felt that his lungs must presently
burst! . . . Then the pressure ceased and he opened
his eyes and saw that his head was sticking out of a
flood of white foam. For a moment he imagined that
the *Ardrossan Castle* had foundered and that he was
floating on the sea, but his arms still gripped the spanker-boom and presently the ship drew herself up and
shook the water from her deck and again ran before
the storm. Morning found them still storm-tossed, with
high seas splashing over the deck, while cold rain and
spume cut their faces. They spent the day in that
state, cold and tired and wet, and at midnight, when
the storm began to abate, they were ordered aloft to
spread sail again. They worked through the night
until a gray light dribbled through a wet sky and they
saw that the sea was falling. The sun came up behind

the heavy clouds, warming them until their gray edges turned white, and presently as the day strengthened itself, the clouds rifted and revealed blue sky.

"Well," said Charlie, as they turned in, "we've had a bit of bad weather!"

Robert, so tired that he felt he could never get refreshed again, smiled at him and replied, "Aye, it was what you might call dirty!"

Charlie looked at him. "If I was choosing a watch," he said, "you're one of the first I'd pick!"

Robert flushed. "Thank you, Charlie!" he said.

THE SECOND CHAPTER

I

THE *Ardrossan Castle* did not immediately return to Glasgow. A chance to carry a bulky cargo to Calcutta tempted her captain, and when that was discharged, he traded for a long while in the China Seas before he returned to Melbourne, after a second visit to Calcutta. They plied for a time in Australian waters, and then set out for Glasgow again. Nearly four years had passed from the day when Robert had fled from the slag-heaps and joined the *Ardrossan Castle* until the day when he stepped ashore at Glasgow again.

"I'm back in this town," said Charlie, "and I'm damned if it isn't still raining! Hi, mister!" he called to a loafer, "has it been raining ever since I went away?"

"How long is it since you left?" the loafer inquired.

"Four years almost!"

"Oh, well, you're unlucky then, for this is the first wet day we've had since you sailed!"

"I'll stand you a pint for that," said Charlie.

They had been paid off and were now free, but jobless, men.

"What I want to do," said Charlie, when they had stowed their dunnage in a Seaman's Shelter, "is to start a chicken farm in the very middle of England, about as far from the smell of the sea as I can get, but what I'm going to do is to take another job on a ship

195

as soon as I've spent all my money! What about you, Darkie?"

"I suppose," Robert replied, "I'll just do the same!"

"Did you ever send that postcard from Melbourne to your mother?"

"No. I suppose I ought to send one to her!"

Charlie nodded, and then said, "Or you could go home?"

"I'll not do that," Robert answered.

But a week later the postcard was still unsent, and when Charlie burst in on Robert one afternoon with the news that two jobs were vacant on an American clipper homeward bound for New York, it was forgotten.

"Some of the hands skipped," said Charlie, "and we're only wanted to go to New York!"

"Right you are," Robert exclaimed.

"The old man's a Blue Nose. So is the first mate!"

Robert had heard appalling stories of the Blue Noses, hard-bitten, harsh seamen from Nova Scotia whose only good quality was their great skill in seamanship. In dog-watches, he had listened incredulously to stories of their cruelties until Charlie had assured him that the worst story he had heard of Blue Noses was probably less terrible than the truth. "A blarsted Blue Nose 'ud murder you for bein' late on your watch!" Ching the Cockney had said, and Charlie, who hated to agree with Ching about anything, agreed that a Blue Nose probably would. Blue Noses laid about them with iron belaying-pins, smashing faces and arms and legs with as little compunction as they would feel in smashing a paper bag. They brutally ill-used apprentices. Charlie had heard of a boy who was tied to the mizzen fife rail for the whole of the time that his ship was beating round the Horn. "The poor little devil nearly died from exposure. He was kept there, half-drowned and miserably cold, day and night, unable to lie down and scarcely able to stand up because the seas broke over him! . . . He did die in the end!"

"Blue Noses'll 'ave a nell all to themselves," Ching asserted. "They won't be allowed to associate with the decent damned!" He himself had been half-killed by a Blue Nose first mate. Ching had been "shanghaied" at 'Frisco. He and the rest of the crew, all dead drunk, were lying in the forecastle, sleeping off the effects of their carouse, when the mate and the second officer came in with iron belaying-pins in their hands and started to sober the crew. "They bleedin' well pulped my fice," Ching said, "an' they killed two chaps! Gawd, if ever I 'ave a Blue Nose in my power I'll knock 'ell out of 'im—an' then I shan't 'ave got 'alf of my own back!"

Charlie interrupted Robert's memories of dog-watch yarns. "Still," he said, "a Blue Nose can't do much if you do your job. And it's only to New York. They're in a hole—nobody in the place will sign on with them—and the pay's good. Coming, Darkie?"

"Are you goin', Charlie?"

Charlie nodded his head.

"All right, then! I'll come, too!" said Robert.

They went down to the river at once and saw the ship, a three-masted California clipper, called the *Blue Dragon,* with fine black sides and a good broad beam. She sat well in the water and seemed a trim and tidy ship.

"Looks well, doesn't she?" said Charlie

Robert, now able to judge a ship, agreed, and Charlie and he went off to see the boarding-master. On the following day, the *Blue Dragon* was towed down the Clyde and, marvellously lucky, they got out to the open sea without the customary beating about the Gareloch. Robert did not like the looks of his mates, among whom was a shivering Arab, and he prayed hard that Charlie and he might be picked for the same watch; they were. The first mate picked them both for the port-watch.

"He is the Bluest Nose I've ever seen," said Charlie, "but I'll bet anything you like he knows his job! I should think his throat will be cut some day or he'll be hanged, or a block will accidentally fall on his head —that Arab looks as if he gave him the jim-jams!—but he knows how to handle a ship—and a crew!"

Robert, regarding the mate's big, blotched, repulsive face with a sense of dread, hoped that the voyage to New York would be swift and short.

II

The *Blue Dragon* was burying her nose in a lop-sided sea, plunging and reeling as the waves hit her sides and splashed on to her decks. Robert felt himself being pushed by the sail he was striving to brace as if it were trying to throw him off. He pressed against it with all his strength, and, so that he might get greater purchase, shifted himself along the yard. He placed his foot on a rope and let his weight rest on it! . . . There was no sound as the rope snapped, for the wind muffled it; he felt his foot drop and he snatched desperately at the sail which bellied against him and pitched him back. His hands scrabbled down the sail as he fell, and his nails felt as if they were being torn from his fingers. He bumped against something and then bumped again, this time on the deck where he lay inert and bleeding. Death had come to him at last; he would be buried at sea and no one belonging to him would ever know what had become of him! . . . Suddenly he felt himself violently jerked from the deck and made to stand up, though his legs seemed to have lost their bones and to be lumps of flabby flesh.

"What in hell," he heard the first mate yelling at him. "What in hell, you God-damned son of a bitch!" He could not understand what was being said of him. The mate's voice foully rattled in his dazed mind. "You try to dodge your job on this ship an' I'll wring your God-damned neck!" Then he was kicked into the forecastle where he lay, stupefied, on the floor. He must already be dead, he thought, and damned. This place was hell. The mate was the Devil. He could hear some one sobbing and he ceased to think about his fate so that he might listen. Some one was suffering even more than he was. He kept quite still so that he might hear—and then he realised that it was he who was sobbing. His body was shaking and sore. The feel of the floor against his face and legs and hands was painful. When he tried to draw one of his legs into a more comfortable position, it hurt him horribly! . . . He wondered how long he would have to lie there. Some one would surely come and attend to him! . . . He could not remember whether a sinner was sent to hell immediately after death or kept in some suspense until the Day of Judgment. The Catholics, of course, believed in Purgatory, but what did the Presbyterians believe? He had not been tried yet—he could

not remember being sentenced to eternal damnation!
. . . Perhaps that was why he was lying on this hard
floor—outside the Judgment Seat. Presently he would
be brought before the Bar of God—he would stand face
to face with Him! . . .

He felt himself being lifted. Some one, whose voice
was familiar, was saying, "All right, Darkie!" It was
Stephens! Had Charlie died and been damned, too?
. . . Were they both about to appear? Charlie was
saying something to him. He must listen to what
Charlie was saying. "What's that, Charlie?" he meant
to say, but his tongue would not utter the words.
But Charlie seemed to know what his thoughts were,
for he repeated his statement. "I shall have to teach
you how to box," he said. Later in the day, so Robert
was told, Charlie made a few remarks to the Blue Nose.
The remarks were perfectly proper and respectful.
"Darkie's unfit for duty for the rest of this trip," he
said. "I'm looking after him," he said, "and he's not
to be disturbed!" The Blue Nose looked at Charlie,
and Charlie looked at the Blue Nose, and neither of
them spoke for a few moments. Then the Blue Nose
spat and walked aft.

III

Robert heard of the affair while he was in hospital.
Charlie and he had signed on for the voyage from
Glasgow to New York, and were paid off on their
arrival in America. Robert, who was immediately
taken to hospital, would have been paid off in any
case because of his accident. Charlie might have signed
on for the trip which the *Blue Dragon* was presently

to make round the Horn to San Francisco, but declined to do so. He had various reasons, he said, for his refusal, and he recited all of them to Robert, who was impressed and puzzled by the last of them. "I believe in discipline at sea," said Charlie.

"What's that got to do with it?" Robert asked.

"A lot," Charlie replied. "I want to have a talk with that Blue Nose about you, and I can't have it while I'm under his orders!"

"Why?"

"It wouldn't be right for a common seaman to talk to his officer in the way I'm going to talk to that Blue Nose. I mean to say, Darkie, it wouldn't be *right!* There must be discipline at sea!"

"What way are you going to talk to him?"

"Oh, just talk to him, you know, as a friend and a brother! Man to man, you know!"

Robert regarded him with suspicion. "You're up to something, Charlie!" he said accusingly.

"Who? Me?" Charlie innocently answered. "Oh, no, Darkie, no! I just want to have a comradely conversation with him—a nice, homely, man-to-man chat."

In a saloon near the East River, Charlie had encountered the mate. The bar was full of seafaring men, and the mate was in the midst of them. Charlie pulled the door open and stood there a few moments, while he looked for his man. His odd behaviour caused the crowd to become silent and nervous. They paused in their drinking to look at him. One of the crew of the *Blue Dragon* recognised him and called out to him, "Close the door, Charlie!" but he ignored the speaker. He found the mate and walked towards him. "Good-morning, Blue Nose!" he said. The mate, insulted, put down his glass of beer on the counter. "What in hell——!" he began.

"One moment, Blue Nose!" Charlie interrupted, "I'm going to say a little piece about you!"

"The hell you are——"

"Manners, Blue Nose, manners! You mustn't interrupt a gentleman when he's making a speech!"

The mate lurched towards him. "You God-damned son of a——!"

"Don't talk about me, Blue Nose! My origin is uninteresting. *You* are the hero of this piece!"

The mate lurched away again, snorting with contempt, though he was aware of the sensation which Charlie's odd behaviour and speech had caused among the other men in the saloon.

"Gentlemen," Charlie continued, "here you see before you a fine, healthy specimen of the Blue Nose! You all know what a Blue Nose is—one of God's gentlest creatures!" There was a roar of laughter at this. "All Blue Noses are members of the Society for the Prevention of Cruelty to Children, and this Blue Nose is the President of the Society!" There was more laughter at this, and the mate, angered by it, suddenly turned and flung a pot of beer at Charlie, who stepped aside only in time to dodge it.

"Naughty little Blue Nose to waste good beer like that!" Charlie said. A flow of pretty speech interrupted. "Tush, tush!" Charlie protested, when the flow had ceased. "Did anybody ever hear such dreadful, dreadful language from a Blue Nose before?" he said, turning to the others. "Whatever will the Christian Endeavour Society in Blue Nose Land say when it hears that this dear brother has spoken profane words——!"

The mate endeavoured to calm himself. "What in hell's your game?" he demanded.

"Game!" Charlie replied. "No game, dear Blue Nose. I've come here to reason with you——!" The mate turned away with a snort of contempt. Charlie continued, addressing the crowd: "This gentle Blue Nose is first mate of the *Blue Dragon*. A pal of mine, a young lad and a good sailor—none of your damn bunt-huggers—and I signed on at Glasgow because nobody else would. Well, my pal was furling a sail in a wind fit to blow your head off—first in the rigging he was! Wasn't he, Blue Nose?"

"Go to hell!"

"Well, gentlemen, you can take my word for that. A rope broke and he fell on the deck and damn near killed himself. And what do you think this gentle Jesus did?"

"I know," said one of the crowd "Picked him up and carried him to the captain's cabin and fed him with chicken broth!"

There was louder laughter at this than at anything else that had been said. Then Charlie told them what the mate had done. "Gawd!" some one said, "ain't Blue Noses horrible!" The mutterings roused the mate to defend himself. "What the hell," he said, "ain't I got to maintain discipline? How d'you think a ship 'ud ever get anywhere if the mate went about molly-coddlin' the crew! Don't you damn well know half the men 'ud dodge their work if the mate didn't hammer hell out of 'em!" The mutterings against him changed to approval of his belief.

"Yes, Blue Nose——!"

"Not so much of the Blue Nose," the mate interrupted.

"You are a Blue Nose, and a pretty little Blue Nose, too. You'd take the first prize in any show of Blue Noses—the champion Blue Nose of the world!"

"Shut your mouth——!"

"In a minute, Blue Nose. All I want to say is that you're a damned rotten mate if you can't tell the difference between a decent sailor and a bunt-hugger! Call yourself an officer when you can't do that! You aren't fit to be a bo'sun, let alone a mate——!"

The mate, now in a rage, roared at him. "Who says I ain't fit to be a mate——?"

"I do. You aren't. You're only fit to be on a cattle-boat. You're only fit to be a bum on a barge. You're no seaman——!"

"I'll wring your blasted neck for that!"

"Wait just another second, Blue Nose. I haven't finished my little piece about you!"

But the mate would hear no more. He came at Charlie, shouting as he came, and instantly there was a ring round both of them.

"Gee, this boy's in for trouble," a man in the crowd called to another, while the bartender came from behind the counter and made ineffective efforts to break through the ring and separate Charlie and the mate. The mate swung his great fist at Charlie's chin and then tried to clinch. "No, little Blue Nose, darling, I want none of your affectionate embraces," Charlie said, jumping aside and landing out with his left as the mate staggered from the force of his own drive. His fist fell on the mate's mouth and sent him reeling back.

"Gawd, that's rattled the Blue Nose a bit!"

The mate recovered himself, and stopped for a minute to take breath and direction. "Don't hurry, Blue Nose," said Charlie tauntingly. "Take your time! Or would you rather quit now? I'm not a boy lying half dead on the deck——!"

The mate came at him again, and this time succeeded in landing his fist on Charlie's body.

"Not bad for you, Blue Nose," Charlie gasped.

"Save your breath, chum!" an English voice called to Charlie.

"He won't have any breath when I've done with him," the mate shouted, swinging round to strike again, but as he did so one of Charlie's fists caught him on the chin and the other drove hard against his heart. "Gee, that lad can punch some!" a sailor said. Charlie did not wait for the mate to recover. He drove again, first with his left full in the mate's face, and again with his right in the same spot, so that the mate felt as if his head were being split in two. Blood was flowing down his face, and one of his eyes was closing! . . . He steadied himself, as he realised that Charlie was a boxer and that he was likely to be beaten through reckless fighting. He moved more warily, though his closing eye made vision difficult for him. The manager of the saloon thrust himself through the ring of onlookers, and, approaching the mate first, ordered him to leave the bar. The mate did not reply; he knocked the manager back into the crowd with a blow that half stunned him. The crowd loudly cheered and laughed.

"It's a pity you can't hit me like that, Blue Nose!" said Charlie, taunting the mate, but the mate refused to be enraged. He came nearer to Charlie and began to feint for an opening, and suddenly he caught Charlie a terrific bang on the jaw. The blow silenced the onlookers. This, they thought to themselves, was punching. The fight was not to be a walk-over for Charlie. The Blue Nose might be a Blue Nose but he could fight. He certainly was game. Give the man his due; he might be and was a bully, but he was no coward. Gee! There he was rushing in again! . . . Missed him, and got a clout on the ear for himself! Gee, that punch would have rattled Charlie all to bits if it had reached where it was meant to reach! . . . The opponents walked round each other, their eyes brilliant with restrained wrath. The mate was breathing very heavily now, and Charlie was beginning to tire. Each realised that he must end the fight quickly if he was to win it. They moved and circled and feinted and then the mate, courageously throwing caution away in the hope that one fierce charge would overwhelm Charlie, jumped in and swung his great fist full at Charlie's face and a moment later he was lying in a crumpled heap on the floor, too dazed to stir. Charlie at the right moment had leaped aside and then, as swiftly as a soldier drives his sword through a man's body, he drove his right fist on to the point of the mate's chin and knocked him senseless to the floor.

"You'll have a pint of beer with us," said one of the onlookers.

"No, thanks," said Charlie, putting on his coat, "I've got to go and visit a pal in hospital!"

" 'E looks as if 'e'd need to be visited in 'ospital too!" an English sailor said, pointing to the mate. "Thank you, chum, 'ooever you are. You've worked off a bit of score for everybody——!"

IV

Robert's stay in hospital was shorter than Charlie or he had imagined it would be. His fall had badly bruised and shaken him, but it had not broken any of his bones; he had been saved from serious injury by various impediments that had, so to speak, lowered him to the deck by degrees. But he was still weak enough, when he was discharged from hospital, to be unfit for an immediate voyage, and so, when Charlie, discussing their plans, proposed that they should beat their way across the continent to California, Robert was glad to agree. They were not short of money. They were, indeed, fairly well off, for they had not remained ashore long enough to melt their money away, and four years' wages, together with the high wages paid to them on the *Blue Dragon,* enabled them to look on the prospect of a spell of unemployment in America without alarm.

"We'll get a ship at 'Frisco easily enough, and at good wages, too. They pay better money out of 'Frisco than anywhere else—and a rest on land'll do us both good!" Charlie concluded.

Robert's heart sank when he learned that San Francisco could not be reached in fewer than six days. "But how'll we pay the fare!" he said.

"What fare?" Charlie replied.

"The railway fare!"

"My God, Darkie, you don't think we're going to pay a *fare!* I'd feel like a passenger if I did that. No, my hearty young sailor, we're going to beat it——!"

Robert did not understand, so Charlie explained.

"We're going to take free and forbidden rides, Darkie! We'll wander down to the station—only be

sure you call it the *de*pot in this God-forsaken country
—and look for a nice comfortable freight train that
happens to be going our way, see! And then we'll
sneak a ride on it when the brakesman isn't looking!''

"That sounds simple!" Robert replied. "Does anybody in America ever pay a fare?"

"Some people do. I ought to tell you that you'll
have to stand on the buffers or lie on top of the wagons,
and if the brakesman comes and catches you, he's very
likely to bump you off, especially if the train's going
full speed. They say that some of these railway com-
panies keep men employed all the year round, just to
go up and down the track collecting the corpses!"

"Ah, quit coddin', Charlie!"

"I mean it, Darkie. Brakesmen think nothing of
killing a chap. As bad as Blue Noses! Who's to
know whether a chap fell off or was pushed off?
Nobody knows who he is—or was—and there are no
sorrowing relatives to claim him or make a fuss about
his death——!"

"Holy O!" said Robert. "D'you mean to say they'd
kill a fella!"

"Without turning a hair!"

"Oh! Well, what's the price of a ticket to California?"

"A terrific lot!"

"Couldn't we get a ship here——?"

"With you as weak as you are!" Charlie said.

Robert reflected and then spoke. "Look here,
Charlie," he said. "I don't want to be a burden to
you!"

"You're no burden to me. Nobody is——!"

"All the same, I know rightly why you're proposin'

this trip to 'Frisco overland when you could easily get a ship here in New York. You don't like leaving me in the lurch!"

"You're absolutely wrong! I'd leave you in the lurch without a minute's hesitation if I wanted to. Don't be sloppy, Darkie. I'm not doing this for your sake. I'm doing it for my own. I want a bit of a rest ashore, and I'd like your company. That's all!"

"You're a hell of a liar, Charlie, but some of your lies are better than that one! Well, all right! I'll give in to you! An' we'll do this beatin' as you call it as soon as you like! When'll we start?"

They did not start at once. Charlie insisted that Robert should recover his strength by staying for a while at a seaside village in Connecticut to which they travelled as paying passengers, since Robert was not yet fit to take free rides. Here they bathed in the surf and lay in the sun, or when the heat became too strong for them, under the shadow of trees or rocks, until Robert felt himself fit again. Then Charlie taught him the science of boxing. "You've got guts," he said during a lesson, "but you've no style. You need both. The chap who taught me used to say that a stout heart and style would take a man through anything anywhere! Come on, man! Put up your dooks!'

"When you're fighting a man, watch his eyes! You can nearly always tell what he is going to do if you watch his eyes. Men who don't know their job always watch the fists, but that's no good. Anybody can deceive you with his fists, but he can't deceive you with his eyes—not often! Now, hit me here—on this spot——!"

Robert tried to hit him there—on that spot, but at

first and for a long while found his fist floundering in the air while he himself was hit there—on that spot. But after a while, his fist floundered less, and then one day it landed there—on that spot, and Charlie staggered back and put up his hand and felt his face.

"Look here, lad," he said, grinning as he spoke, "you're getting a bit above yourself! Do you know that you hit me? Yes, and you damn well hurt me, too!" His tone altered slightly. "You can punch, Darkie!" he said admiringly.

Their boxing attracted crowds, so they resolved to practise in less frequented places. They found a natural "ring" in a wood more than a mile from the town; a flat grassy patch surrounded by trees and bushes where they could box unobserved. It was in this place that they met Lop Ear. They came one morning along the path, so narrow that they had to walk in single file, that led to the "ring," and there in the centre of it found Lop Ear, an oddly, but almost stylishly, dressed man, who was cooking a meal by a wood fire. His coat was made of tweed and his trousers of brown linen; his boots were excellent but unpolished; and his collarless shirt seemed only to have been put on that morning. He was neater than either Charlie or Robert were. His hair was short and tidy and his face was cleanly shaved. His hands were soft-looking and his nails were trim. He looked at the intruders at first with interest and then with resentment.

"Good-morning!" Charlie said.

The stranger nodded his head and moved nearer to the fire. A delicious smell of coffee came from the can on it.

"Pic-nicking?" Charlie continued.

"Pic-*what?*" It was then that his interest in them changed to resentment.

"I thought perhaps you were having a little holiday or something," Charlie said nervously.

"Say, air you presoomin' to be funny?"

"No, I—I—I beg your pardon!"

Robert stared at Charlie in amazement, for Charlie appeared to be embarrassed. He was stammering!

"I suppose you guys is havin' a holiday!" said the stranger.

"Not exactly! My pal's been sick—in hospital, so we'd thought we'd stay here until he got better. Then we're going to beat it to California!"

Instantly the demeanour of the stranger altered. The look of resentment left his face and he became genial again. "Gee," he said, "I thought you was guys that worked. Sit down an' have some cawfee!"

They did as they were bid, and presently were sharing an extraordinary meal, which the stranger produced from parcels that were concealed in his clothes; meat, sandwiches, chops, cakes, bread and butter, a large pie and very good coffee, the smell of which, when they had first entered the "ring," had immediately made them feel hungry. Their host informed them that he was known throughout the whole of Connecticut as Lop Ear, and he drew their attention to the disproportion between his ears which accounted for his nickname. They had only to mention his name to most any one in Connecticut and they would be well and even lavishly treated. Connecticut was the part of America he knew best, but he had beat his way from the Canadian border to the Gulf of Mexico, from the Atlantic to the Pacific, and there sure was nothing anybody could tell him about the United States! He poured out a flood of talk and gave them no opportunity to reply to the questions that occasionally he put to them. He reckoned that the life they led was the finest life of all. Gee, when he thought of the guys that worked! . . . It kinda 'curred to him, though, that if there wasn't any guys in the world who were willin' to work, it 'ud go darned hard with people like Lop Ear! . . . The thought, as it sank deeper into his mind, seemed to frighten him. "Gee," he said apprehensively and more to himself than to them, "I hope no one don't go an' tell them to stop workin'!" He reflected again and seemed to find comfort in his new thought. "But I reckon some folks must like work! They must do! They wouldn't work if they didn't! Gee, that's queer!"

"What's queer?" Robert asked.

"People likin' to work! I never done no work in my life, an' I airn't never likely to do none. Gee, I'd feel ashamed to work! If my parents was to catch me workin', it 'ud break their hearts——!"

Robert's Ulster traditions were being outraged by Lop Ear's talk. "Are you a tramp?" he said indignantly.

"Why, of course. Only we calls them hobos in this country. Airn't youse guys tramps, too!" The look of suspicion reappeared in his eyes as he spoke.

"No, we aren't!" said Robert. "We're sailors——!"

Lop Era sprang to his feet. "Say," he said, "I thought you was the same as me, an' you was workin' men all the while. Boys, that airn't decent. You've deceived me! I'd have given you a meal if you'd told me the truth, but I wouldn't have let you sit here talkin' to me like friends if I'd knowed you was workin' men! Youse've indooced me to treat youse like hobos, and all the while youse air workers! That aren't decent, boys! You've took advantage of me——!"

Robert stared at Charlie, who began to laugh.

"Be the holy fly!" said Roger, unable to control himself any longer. "D'you mean to sit there an' say we ought to be ashamed of ourselves for workin'——!"

"Youse ought to be ashamed of youseselves for passin' youseselves as honest hobos when youse airn't nothin' but workin' men! Youse kin work if youse want to, but you airn't got no right to associate with folks what don't. I take it real hard of you to abuse my cawnfidence——!"

Robert said "Holy O!" and subsided, while Charlie lay back and roared with laughter.

"Gee, it airn't nothin' to leff at!" Lop Ear complained.

"I'm sorry, Lop Ear," Charlie apologised. "But I don't see that we can do anything——!"

"If youse was to say youse air sorry, that wouldn't be so bad, but to leff——!" He paused for a moment or two and then hurriedly said, "If youse was to give up workin'——!"

"What!" said Robert.

"Repent and be saved!" Charlie said.

"Yeh, that's the ticket! Repent an' be saved!" Lop Ear eagerly exclaimed. "Make up youse mind how you airn't gonna do no more work as long's as youse live unless youse is compelled to an' kain't help youseselves——!"

"Be a damned tramp!" Robert angrily exclaimed.

Lop Ear gazed at him reproachfully. "You sure air young an' headstrong," he said.

"Darkie's damn nearly dead in his sin, Lop Ear!" Charlie said apologetically. "But I daresay the sinner can be saved——!"

"I don't like this sort of talk," Robert said to Charlie. Charlie ignored him. "You'll hardly believe me," he continued to Lop Ear, "I've seen that chap offering to do other people's work!"

"Gee!" said Lop Ear in what might be called horror.

"That will show you how far gone he is. You'll have a hard job to make a tramp of him!"

"Nobody in this world'll ever do that," Robert said.

"Listen to him, Lop Ear! He's a hardened worker!"

Lop Ear leant forward and began to tell Robert his history. "My parents was hobos, an' so was their parents. It must be over a hundred years since anybody in our family worked. I reckon I got a reputation to live up to! There airn't many old families in America, but I belong to one of them, an' I kin tell you right here an' now I airn't gonna disgrace it—not by workin' I airn't. An' if you wanna keep good with me you gotta stop workin'. I airn't gonna be seen walkin' about with guys that work!"

Robert rose to his feet. "Come on, Charlie," he said sarcastically, "we aren't fit company for his lord god almightiness!"

Charlie took hold of his coat-tail and pulled him down again. "Wait a minute," he said. "Look here, Lop Ear," he continued, "we can promise you something; we won't do any work in America!"

"Well, I reckon that's better'n nothin'——!"

"You can't promise that, Charlie. You said yourself

we were goin' to pick fruit somewhere!" Robert interrupted.

"Except a little fruit-picking!" Charlie continued. "I hope, Lop Ear, that is not against your principles!"

"Well, I don't know. It's darned nearly work. My grandfather never done no fruit-pickin', but my father called it recreation! I wouldn't pick none myself, but I reckon it's a matter of conscience. If youse can pick fruit with a clear conscience then I reckon youse air entitled to pick it! I don't know as my conscience 'ud let me do it——!"

"You see, Lop Ear," said Charlie, "Darkie isn't quite better yet, and I thought fruit-picking would just put him right!"

"I get your point, Charlie. It airn't work; it's medicine! That makes a difference!"

"He'll probably eat more than he picks," Charlie added.

Lop Ear was now reconciled to the idea that his new friends should pick fruit. He even hinted that he might pick a berry or two himself. "They's fruit farms up in Michigan," he said. "Why don't you guys beat it up there with me? You kin easy beat it from Chicago to California."

"We will," said Charlie. "Tell us what to do!"

"Youse leave it to me," said Lop Ear, preparing to pack up.

"How far is it to Chicago?" Robert asked.

"About a thousand miles!" Charlie replied.

"Sufferin' Jases! Are we goin' to stand on buffers all that far?"

"No, sir!" Lop Ear said. "Not all in one spell. We'll step off at places where there's a good jail!"

"A good what?" Robert shouted.

"Jail!" Lop Ear repeated. "I know some good jails——!"

"D'you mean to say you can walk into a jail for the night?" Robert demanded.

"Sure!"

Robert opened his mouth to speak, but words would not come.

"Gee, I know jails where they pay you to go in," Lop Ear continued. "I go reg'lar to some of them, but I never stay more'n a month in any of them. I get tired of bein' in the same place for long!"

Robert gulped and gasped. "Charlie," he said, "I thought you were the champion liar of the world, but you've got to hand it to Lop Ear. He'd make Ananias feel like—like——!"

"George Washington," Charlie suggested.

But Lop Ear paid no heed to them. When he had stowed the food in his clothes, he said, "I'll see you at the *de*-pot. They's a empty truck standin' in the side track. If youse get there after dark an' wait for me 'til I come, youse'll be all right!"

v

Lop Ear was waiting for them at the depot. His body seemed to be bulkier than it was when he left them in the morning, and indeed it was, for he had spent part of the day in begging for food, great quantities of which were stowed in various parts of his clothes.

"What do you do for it?" Robert asked.

"Do!" Lop Ear exclaimed.